"PROMISES OF LOVE"

"Love the story. Love the fact the word goes thru the story in everyday situations as it should in our lives. When you finish you are blessed." *Sue Winder*

"This was a wonderful story, Harrison and Zoe was so much in love and I could not put the book down, hard to see the end. A must read!" *Pauline James*

"This is my favourite book so far by Juliette Duncan. I was never sure how the story would end and I loved all the twists and surprises she added into the story. This is definitely a must read book. You don't need to read any of the other books to follow this story as it is a stand-alone book." *Ann*

"I really enjoyed this beautiful story of God who never leaves or forsakes us no matter the circumstances a God who really cares and understands us and Who is also the prayer answerer" *Ann*

"I love this book. The author has woven things that we deal with in our daily lives into a story of love and faith. It's the story of two people who find each other and fall in love but have lots of challenges to face along the way to their wedding. Anyone that loves to read good Christian love stories, will love this book. The author is so good about developing the characters so that readers feel like they really know and connect with them." *Mary Stanake*

"This book has it all! The characters seemed so real that I laughed, cried, worried, and rejoiced along with them. A wonderful story with a great message!" *EN*

"What a wonderful book. It shares our humanness, our fears, our struggles, and our delights. I love the use of scripture and the calling God had for each one of us." *Ddmost*

Other Books by Juliette Duncan

Contemporary Christian Romance

The Shadows Trilogy

Lingering Shadows
Facing the Shadows
Beyond the Shadows
(The Sequel) Secrets and Sacrifice

The True Love Series

Tender Love
Tested Love
Tormented Love
Triumphant Love
True Love at Christmas

Promises of Love

Middle Grade Christian Fiction

The Madeleine Richards Series

Rebellion in Riversleigh
Problems in Paradise
Trouble in Town

PROMISES

OF

LOVE

A CONTEMPORARY CHRISTIAN ROMANCE

Juliette Duncan

Cover Design by http://www.StunningBookCovers.com

Chapter One

Brisbane, Australia

When Zoe Taylor's alarm clock buzzed on the morning after Christmas, she stretched her hand out and hit 'snooze' and drifted back to sleep. A moment later she sat with a start—Harrison would be here in less than half an hour. Rubbing the sleep from her eyes, the brand new, white gold engagement ring on her finger caught her eye. A warm glow spread through her body as she held her hand out, allowing the diamond to sparkle in the early morning sunlight. Fancy Harrison proposing to her in front of his entire family and friends during their Christmas celebrations at his parents' place yesterday afternoon! Exhaling a long sigh of contentment, Zoe's heart warmed with love for Harrison.

She slipped out of bed, showered, and dressed in the outfit she'd selected the night before—a pair of white shorts and the lightest shirt she owned—a striped blue and white sleeveless T. Following a quick scan of the apartment in case she'd forgotten something, Zoe grabbed her bag and headed downstairs just as Harrison's sports car turned the corner.

Her heart quickened as Harrison jumped out of the car and strode towards her. His smile was wide, his teeth strikingly white against the brown stubble on his face. As he lifted her off the ground and spun her around, nearly dropping her, joy bubbled from deep within and she laughed out loud. Could life get any better?

He lowered her to the ground and brushed her hair with his hand, gazing deeply into her eyes before kissing her slowly.

Zoe melted into his arms and lost herself in his embrace before remembering where she was. Tearing herself away, she stifled a giggle. "What will the neighbours say?"

Harrison glanced left, then right. "I don't see any, do you?"

Zoe chuckled. "No."

He lowered his lips again, and by the time he finished, Zoe was breathless and flushed.

Her chest heaved. "We need to get going, Harrison."

"Can't we go inside?"

Mixed feelings surged through her. How could she keep her resolve with Harrison's soft brown eyes looking at her like that? As she lifted her hand and gently stroked the stubble on his cheek, she willed her heart to remain strong. "No, Harrison. I told you last night. I want to wait until we're married."

Harrison's bottom lip protruded in a pout and he looked at her with puppy dog eyes.

Zoe chuckled. "You'll trip over it if you're not careful." Stretching up, she slipped her hand around Harrison's neck, and gently pulling his head towards her, brushed her lips across his. "I'll make sure it's worth the wait."

"It's going to kill me, you know that."

The sweetness of his breath tickled her senses. She laughed. "No, it won't." Placing a quick kiss on his lips, she pulled away. "Besides, we need to get going. Mum and Dad are expecting us for lunch."

Harrison's shoulders slumped as he let out a resigned sigh. "Best get going, then." Leaning down, he picked up Zoe's bag and placed it in the boot beside his before opening the passenger door of the car and holding it open for her. Zoe laughed as he stole another kiss before she slipped under his arm and onto the soft leather seat of his fancy new convertible.

Harrison slid in beside her and raised his brow as he glanced at the roof. "Up or down?"

"Need you ask?" Zoe laughed again as she positioned her cap on her head, pulling her pony tail through the hole in the back.

"No." Chuckling, Harrison flicked the switch and the top folded down. He turned the key in the ignition, bringing the car to life, and accelerated down the tree lined street. If the neighbours hadn't been awake before, they would be now.

They soon left the bustle of the city behind. Hot wind pulled at Zoe's thin shirt and whipped loose hair around her chin as they sped along the country highway, heading north-west towards her parents' property. A thin haze of smoke from distant bush fires hung in the air and began burning Zoe's throat. She sipped her water, but finally asked Harrison to close the roof.

"At least we can talk now." Harrison slipped his hand onto Zoe's leg and raised his brow, one side of his mouth lifting in a playful grin.

Chuckling, Zoe raised her hand and inspected her ring. "Guess we can."

"Like it?" Harrison had one eye on the road and one eye on her.

Zoe nodded, a smile pulling at the corners of her mouth. "I love it."

"I'm glad." Harrison's voice was warm and gentle as his hand moved slowly up her leg.

Zoe slapped his hand playfully—he wasn't going to make it easy for her. Maybe it didn't matter, after all, she and Harrison would be married before long. But no, how could she go against all she'd been taught? Maybe she'd let her faith slip of late, but she knew what was right and what was wrong. And

3

this was wrong. Surely Harrison knew it too, having been brought up by Christian parents. Was he just testing her?

"So, when can we get married?" Harrison raised both his brows expectantly as he gently caressed her leg.

Zoe laughed again, she couldn't help it. He was just like a little kid sometimes, but she loved him, especially when he looked at her like that. Before she could answer, the car skidded off the road. Gravel sprayed into the air as it spun out of control. Zoe screamed and held on, her heart thumping. When would it stop? Her heart raced. What were they going to hit?

Harrison gripped the wheel with both hands, struggling to regain control. Gradually he brought the car to a stop. Leaning his head against the steering wheel, he sucked in quick breaths.

After several seconds he raised his head. "Sorry, Zoe." He spoke quietly, meekly.

Zoe's chest heaved. "You could have killed us." Her hand shook against her chest, and she could barely speak.

"I know. I'm sorry. It was careless of me." Harrison turned his head and met her gaze. Releasing a long sigh, he drew her close and kissed the top of her hair as he stroked her face with his fingers. "I really am sorry, Zoe."

They weren't hurt and it was silly to stay angry. Exhaling slowly, Zoe lifted her face and looked into his eyes. "Just keep your eyes on the road in the future."

He gave her a hang dog look. "I will. I've been suitably chastised."

"Good."

Harrison took her hand and pressed it to his lips. "I love you, Zoe."

Zoe's heart softened. How could she stay angry at him?

A sheepish grin grew on his face. "You didn't answer my question."

Zoe chuckled as she shook her head. "I don't know. When were you thinking?"

"Easter, perhaps?"

Zoe's eyes widened. "Easter? How could we organise a wedding that soon?"

Harrison ran his fingers down her hairline, tucking some stray hair behind her ear. "You don't know my mum."

"But *we* need to organise and plan it, Harrison, not your mum."

"You're right. But she'll want to be involved."

Zoe blew out a breath. To be honest, no way could she think about organising a wedding any time soon, with or without help from either of their mothers—her Internship began in two weeks. She angled her head. "Could we wait until next year?"

Harrison's head jolted up. "Next year?" His eyebrows puckered. "That's ages away, Zoe."

She gazed into his disappointed eyes. "I know, but I've got a really busy year, Harrison. You know that."

Harrison's shoulders slumped as he exhaled slowly. "Yes, I do know that." He rubbed his thumb along the top of her hand. "I'm sorry, Zoe, I'll try to be patient, but that's a really long time."

She smiled at him. "It'll go quickly, you'll see."

"I hope so." Leaning forward, he cupped his hand around her face and kissed her gently.

As Zoe melted into Harrison's arms, waves of warmth flowed through her. Reluctantly, she finally pulled away. "We'd better be going, Harrison."

He glanced at the clock on the dash. "Guess you're right." Sighing heavily, he straightened in his seat and engaged first gear before pulling back onto the road.

For the next few minutes, Zoe sat in silence with her hand on his leg. It *was* going to be a long year. As much as she wanted to marry Harrison, she just had too much on her plate. And besides, his proposal had been totally unexpected, catching her off-guard, so he couldn't really expect her to drop everything and plan a wedding, could he? Zoe sighed. Maybe she was being selfish.

As she studied Harrison's profile, a smile grew on Zoe's face. This handsome, clever, caring man was going to be her husband—what a lucky girl she was.

Harrison glanced at her. "So what reason did your folks give for not making it to the city?"

Zoe's smiled slipped as she let out a sigh. The reason Mum gave when she called yesterday didn't ring true, and it had been puzzling her. Being country folk, her parents avoided the city as much as they could, but to call off their trip at the last minute because of a problem with a pump? That didn't sound right. Dad could fix things like that. She shrugged. "I'm not really sure. I got the feeling Mum wasn't telling me something."

Harrison's eyebrows drew together. "Like what?"

"I don't know. Guess we'll find out soon."

Chapter Two

As Harrison and Zoe approached the tiny town of Bellhaven a few hours later, Zoe's eyes widened. The country was in drought, but when had it got this bad? Undulating hills, normally covered in green grass and cattle, were now brown and dry. The few cattle still grazing were skin and bone and Zoe's heart went out to them as they struggled to find enough to eat.

The tall gum trees lining either side of the main street offered some shade, but the leaves looked parched, and the garden beds, normally filled with brightly coloured annuals, lay empty. Why hadn't Mum told her how bad it was?

The main street was also empty. All the shops were shut, not entirely unexpected given it was the day after Christmas, but what caught Zoe's attention were the number of shops permanently closed. Even the Haberdashery store, one of the original shops in town, was boarded up. Poor Mrs. Sullivan. The store had been the kindly lady's life. Zoe smiled as she remembered the brightly coloured ribbons Mrs. Sullivan always brought out when Zoe popped in after school.

Harrison glanced at Zoe as he slowed the car even further. "Does it always look like this?"

Zoe shook her head. "I had no idea it was so bad." She bit her lip. She'd been so busy this past year she hadn't visited her parents for months. They'd be struggling if this was anything to go by.

'Bellrae', her parents' farm, was only five minutes the other side of town. Harrison slowed and indicated left under Zoe's direction before turning. She breathed a sigh of relief as they drove up the long driveway bordered on either side by rows of citrus trees. At first glance the orange trees looked green and healthy, perhaps just a little smaller, but as Zoe took a closer look, she noticed many of the leaves were curled. She tried to ignore the sick feeling growing in her stomach.

She shifted her gaze to the farmhouse in front of them. Wide verandahs wrapped around three sides. Bougainvillea in a range of vivid pinks and oranges grew either side of the front steps, providing some respite from the relentless sun. At least something was flourishing. Several large sheds bulged with farm equipment.

The poinciana tree to the right of the house was also surviving, and continued to provide the deep shade the whole family sought on days like this, but the grass underneath was no longer green and soft. Mum had never let it go like this the whole time they'd lived here, until now.

As Harrison brought the car to a halt in front of the house, the front screen door flew open and Mum appeared, face flushed and glistening with perspiration, wiping her hands on her apron as she waved from the top of the steps.

Opening the car door, Zoe gasped, the air hot and heavy as she struggled for breath. Trying to ignore it, she lifted her hand and waved.

"Zoe, Harrison, welcome! Merry Christmas" Mum bustled down the steps and held her arms out to Zoe.

Smiling broadly, Zoe gave Mum a long hug. "Merry Christmas to you too, Mum." She planted a kiss on Mum's flushed cheek and then, waving a hand in front of her face, stepped back. "But it's so hot!"

Mum nodded, blowing some hair off her damp cheek. "Yes, and no change in sight, I'm afraid." She turned and held her arms out to Harrison. "Merry Christmas, Harrison."

Harrison smiled and returned her hug. "And to you, Mrs. Taylor."

Mum gave a dismissive wave of her hand and chuckled. "Call me Ruth. No formalities out here. Come inside and I'll get you both a drink." She stopped all of a sudden and lifted Zoe's left hand. "Zoe! What's this on your finger?"

Zoe bit her lip as she tried to contain her smile. She'd meant to remove her ring so she and Harrison could break the news to her parents together. How could she have forgotten? She relaxed and smiled into Mum's surprised eyes as she slipped her arm around Harrison's waist. "We're engaged, Mum. We were planning on telling you and Dad when we got inside."

Mum's eyes misted over as she squeezed Zoe's hand and drew her into a big hug. "Congratulations, Zo." Pulling a tissue from her apron pocket, she dabbed her eyes before hugging Harrison again.

"We didn't mean to spring it on you like that, Mum." Zoe lifted her gaze to meet Harrison's and flashed him a smile. "Harrison proposed yesterday, and we wanted to tell you in person."

Harrison placed his arm around Zoe's shoulder and pulled her close, kissing the top of her head.

"Well, I'm happy for you both." Mum's eyes glistened. "Now come inside out of this heat."

Zoe and Harrison followed Mum up the stairs and into the house. Nothing had changed since her last visit. The long hallway down the centre of the house leading to the kitchen at the back was lined with black and white photographs of family members past and present. Zoe glanced into the formal lounge room on the right—nothing different there either. The floral lounge suite had perhaps faded a little more, but apart from that, it looked the same as always—comfortable but old.

"Where's Dad?" Zoe asked when they reached the kitchen.

"He'll be here in a minute. He's just cleaning up for lunch."

Mum turned the ceiling fan up a notch but it only moved more of the hot air around.

"Still no air-conditioning?" Zoe asked as she took a seat and fanned her face with a Christmas card she picked up off the kitchen dresser.

Mum shook her head, her expression slipping. "No, just the fan, sorry." Turning to Harrison, her face brightened. "Harrison, what can I get you to drink?"

"Just water, thanks." Beads of perspiration sat on Harrison's forehead.

Mum took a jug of cold water from the fridge and poured a glass. "Zoe?"

"The same, thanks Mum. It's too hot for anything else."

"Ah, here's Dad!" Mum's face lit up as Dad entered the room.

Zoe stood and stepped towards him. "Merry Christmas, Dad."

"Merry Christmas, Zo." Extending his arms, he drew her into a tight embrace.

When Zoe stepped away, Harrison stood and held out his hand. "Merry Christmas, Mr. Taylor."

Dad grasped Harrison's hand with both of his. "And to you, Harrison, but please call me Kevin." The smile on his face and the tone of his voice were genuine. "How was your trip?"

"Hot." Harrison chuckled, sending a quick glance to Zoe.

Mum poured another glass of water and placed it on the table in front of Dad.

"Thanks, love." Dad's eyes crinkled at the edges as he smiled at her. Zoe's heart warmed. Would she and Harrison

10

still look at each other like that after they'd been married almost forty years? She hoped so.

Sitting down beside Dad, Mum placed her elbows on the table and leaned forward, her hazel eyes lighting up. "You'd better tell Dad your news."

Dad looked up, his eyebrows drawing together.

Zoe turned her head, angling it slightly as she held Harrison's gaze. Who was going to tell Dad?

Straightening, Harrison cleared his throat. He slipped his arm around Zoe's shoulder and pulled her close.

Zoe's heart thumped. She sucked in a breath. Maybe Harrison should have asked Dad first... *maybe he had?*

"Kevin, Ruth," Harrison glanced at one and then the other, "I've come to love your daughter very much." His voice was steady and strong. Zoe released her nervous breath.

Turning his head, Harrison's smile reached deep inside her. "Yesterday I asked Zoe to marry me, and she said yes."

Zoe waited for a response. Her heart raced. She searched Harrison's eyes. Why was Dad taking so long to say anything? The silence was killing her. She tore her gaze away from Harrison and turned slowly to look at Dad.

Dad removed his glasses and placed them on the table. He stood and shook Harrison's hand before reaching out for Zoe and hugging her. When he released her, his eyes glistened and he looked like he might cry.

Standing behind Dad, Mum placed her hands on his shoulders and squeezed gently.

Something was amiss. Zoe angled her head. "What's wrong?"

Dad lowered his head and brushed his eyes with the back of his hand.

Zoe drew her eyebrows together. "Mum?"

Mum's shoulders sagged as she blinked back tears. "We were trying to keep it from you, Zoe."

"Keep what, Mum? Is Dad sick?" Zoe's gaze darted between her parents.

Mum's eyes shot open. "No, nothing like that."

Zoe sighed with relief. "Well, what is it?"

Mum sat down and squeezed Dad's hand. "We're in trouble, Zoe. Financial trouble." Dad's thumb rubbed circles on Mum's hand. The clock's tick grew louder.

"We're probably going to lose the farm." Mum's voice caught, her hand flying to her mouth.

Zoe's eyes popped. Had she heard right? *Her parents were going to lose the farm? How could that happen after all these years?* "I…I don't understand. How?"

Dad lifted his head and drew a deep breath. "A combination of things, Zo. The floods last year destroyed a lot of the crop, and now we've been in drought this year, as well as a few other things."

Zoe leaned forward. "What other things?"

Dad's eyes moistened again. "It's my fault, Zoe. I made some bad investment decisions."

"No, Kevin, it was both our doing." Mum squeezed Dad's wrist and peered into his eyes.

Zoe's mouth was dry. She swallowed hard. *This can't be happening. It's a bad dream.* But it wasn't—she was wide awake. "How much did you lose, Dad?"

Dad grimaced. "A lot."

A lump grew in Zoe's stomach. "That's unlike you, Dad. You're normally so careful."

Dad drew another slow breath. "We thought it was a good deal, but turned out it wasn't."

Zoe shook her head. "What made you do it?"

"We were investing for our future, and got caught." Dad sounded so sad as he gently squeezed Zoe's wrist.

Zoe's heart ached for him. They'd worked so hard to keep the farm afloat. It was their life. They couldn't lose it now.

Dad picked up his glasses and slipped them back on. "Grandma will be here soon, so let's have lunch and we can talk about it later, sweetheart."

"Doesn't Grandma know?" Zoe held Dad's gaze. Grandma would be devastated, but surely she had a right to know—after all, it was her home, too.

Dad shook his head. "Not the full story."

Zoe released a sad sigh. "Okay, let's leave it for now, but why didn't you tell me?"

Mum squeezed Zoe's wrist. "We're sorry, Zoe. We've been trusting God for a solution, but we're still waiting. We hoped you wouldn't need to know."

Zoe blew out a breath, her shoulders sagging. If only they'd trusted God to provide for their future instead of making some dodgy investment. As soon as the thought entered her head, she chastised herself. No need to be judgmental. They must have thought they were doing the right thing, otherwise they wouldn't have done it. But would God give them money to fix their mistake?

Zoe searched Mum's eyes. "Does Peter know?"

Mum nodded. "He heard us talking about it and now he's upset."

Of course her brother would be upset. No way would Peter, with his Down's Syndrome, understand how Mum and Dad could lose their home.

A soft knock sounded on the back door and Grandma poked her head in.

Mum quickly rubbed her face with her hands.

Dad blew his nose.

Zoe squeezed Harrison's hand and planted a smile on her face as she stood and walked to the door. "Grandma, Merry Christmas!" Leaning forward, she wrapped her arms around Grandma's frail shoulders and gave her a gentle hug.

"Oh Zoe, my dear, it's lovely to see you." Her voice sounded so sweet. "And my, look at your beautiful hair! How do you keep it so nice?" Grandma's eyes sparkled as she reached up and touched Zoe's auburn hair.

Zoe chuckled. "Grandma, you always say that!"

"Do I, dear? I'm sorry." She began patting Zoe's hand, but within a moment, she stopped and drew it closer. "And what's this I see?"

Zoe laughed. She'd almost forgotten. "It didn't take you long, Grandma! But yes…" she glanced at Harrison and caught his eye. "Harrison and I are engaged."

Grandma's face lit up. "A wedding! How wonderful!"

Zoe returned Grandma's smile, but inside, her heart crumbled. How could she and Harrison be planning a wedding when her parents were facing financial ruin and their whole life could be turned upside down?

Chapter Three

"That was a lovely lunch, thanks, Mum." Placing her knife and fork together on her plate, Zoe gave Mum a grateful smile. It was so hard trying to pretend everything was all right in front of Grandma, but a few things Grandma said every now and then suggested she was more aware of the situation than Mum or Dad knew.

Zoe kept an open ear and eye throughout the meal. Dad was putting on a brave face, but his hands, normally steady and strong, held a slight tremor, and his face looked strained. Not surprising if he was about to lose everything he'd worked for, even if he and Mum were trusting God like they said.

Mum talked too much, even more than normal. Peter sat beside Harrison and asked lots of questions about animals. Being a vet, Harrison was in his element, but Peter could be intense at times, and Harrison shot the occasional glance at Zoe as if he was wanting to be rescued. She just laughed.

Grandma, as sweet as ever, just sat there talking quietly to everyone, asking questions, nodding, listening.

Maybe Peter had told Grandma, and she was just pretending she didn't know? It wouldn't surprise her.

Mum began scraping the dirty plates. "We're planning a visit to Uncle Stephen's and Aunt Veronica's this afternoon, Zoe. Would you and Harrison like to join us?"

What could she say? They really had no choice, although

she'd rather have a discussion about her parents' financial situation. Zoe drew her eyebrows together. Did Uncle Stephen know? If he did, surely he'd help his brother out. He wouldn't just stand by and watch her parents lose the farm that had been in the family for generations, would he? A sinking feeling grew in her stomach. Maybe they were struggling too and needed help themselves.

Zoe smiled at Mum again. "That would be lovely, Mum. I'm looking forward to seeing them and the new baby." But not knowing the full details played heavily on Zoe. Maybe she could get some time alone with Mum by helping with the dishes. "Let me help, Mum." Zoe stood and began collecting the condiments before Mum could tell her not to. Following Mum into the kitchen, she placed the tray on the kitchen counter and then turned around and folded her arms. "So, how bad is it really, Mum? Be honest."

"I'd rather you didn't know." Mum turned on the tap and began rinsing plates.

"I'd like to know." Zoe's voice softened.

Mum lifted her head and looked out the window, her hands resting on the edge of the sink. "If we don't make next month's loan payment, the bank will foreclose."

So soon? Zoe's heart raced. "And how much is that?" She held her breath. She had no idea how much their payments were, but guessed they were huge.

"You really don't want to know." Mum turned around slowly, her eyes misting over.

"How much, Mum?" Zoe's heart thudded as she waited.

Mum drew in a big breath before lifting her head and meeting Zoe's gaze. "Ten thousand."

Zoe gasped, her eyes widening. "Ten thousand? That's huge, Mum. How did it get so big?"

Mum wiped her eyes with her apron. "The bank let us miss a few payments, but now they're wanting us to catch up."

She struggled to speak.

Zoe's brows knitted. "That doesn't seem right."

Mum gave a helpless shrug. "They won't budge."

"And you don't have the money?"

Mum shook her head.

"Surely they won't turn you out?"

Mum grimaced. "They will if we don't come up with it."

Zoe squared her shoulders. She couldn't believe what she was hearing. "But you've been with them for years."

"It doesn't matter, Zoe. They know we don't have any money."

Stepping forward, Zoe placed her hands on Mum's arms. "Let me help, Mum."

Mum shook her head. "No, Zoe. You've got your own future to think of."

"Let me decide that. But first I need to know if there's any chance of getting your money back." She paused. She didn't want to pry, but if she didn't know, she couldn't help. "What did you invest in, Mum?"

"Best sit down." Mum pulled out a chair and sat. Sadness clouded her face as she lifted her gaze to Zoe's. "A man Dad had known for years told us about some property investments he said were guaranteed to make money." She swallowed hard as tears flooded her eyes. "We believed him and mortgaged the farm to buy in." She sucked in a deep breath and looked down at her hands. "And we also invested money in a company he recommended."

Zoe reached out and squeezed Mum's hand as a heavy weight settled in her stomach. This was worse than she'd thought. How had they let themselves get talked into doing something like this? "And there's no chance of getting it back?"

Mum shook her head. "The man disappeared. Turned out he was a scammer and he ran off with the money. No-one's heard of him since."

"Surely something can be done?"

Mum shrugged. "We've tried."

Zoe's mind raced. This was so unfair. "What about the income from the farm?"

More tears welled in Mum's eyes. "Two bad years in a row, and we don't have enough money to keep the water up to the trees or to feed the cattle."

"And the bank won't lend you any more money?"

"No." Mum dabbed her eyes, her body shuddering as she sucked in a deep breath. "I'm sorry, Zoe. Normally I'm okay." She smiled through her tears. "I know God will provide for us. We just have to be patient and trust Him."

Mum's faith had always been strong, but Zoe wasn't sure what God could do to save the farm when it seemed He only had a couple of weeks to do it. A miracle was needed, but how often did miracles like that happen these days? Maybe Mum's faith was too simple.

Zoe took Mum's hand and squeezed it. "While you're waiting for God, I'm going to help, and you can't stop me."

Tears rolled down Mum's cheek as Zoe leaned forward and wrapped her arms around her.

Later that night, after they'd visited Uncle Stephen and Aunt Veronica and met Zoe's new cousin, Ivy, and played some outdoor games with the other three children, Zoe told Harrison what Mum had said. "I want to help them, Harrison. I don't know what I can do, but I'd hate for them to lose the farm."

"It's a huge amount of money they owe, Zoe. And that's just one month."

Zoe sighed as she gazed up at the half moon. "I know. They've really got themselves in a mess." It was just horrible and she felt sick in her stomach just thinking about it.

"Have they got anything they can sell?"

Zoe tilted her head. "Like machinery and stuff?"

Harrison nodded.

"Maybe. We can ask." Zoe leaned back on the bench seat and snuggled into Harrison's arms. She almost felt guilty sitting here like this while her parents' world crumbled around them. She and Harrison had their whole future ahead of them. Harrison had a promotion, albeit temporary while Tessa, the clinic manager, was away, and when she finished her Internship, Zoe would be earning good money as a doctor, but right now, her income wasn't enough to get her parents out of trouble.

Zoe rubbed her arms. It always cooled down out here at night... why hadn't she remembered her jacket? She laughed to herself. A good excuse to snuggle closer.

She picked at the light brown hairs on Harrison's arm. "I've got some money saved—I'd like to give them some."

Harrison twiddled some of her loose hair between his fingers. "You need to think carefully before you do, Zoe. You've worked hard for that money."

Harrison wasn't wrong. Working part-time to support herself while also studying full-time had been a hard slog, but somehow she'd managed to save a reasonable amount.

She sat up. "I can't let them lose the farm, Harrison. I've got to do something."

"You're right, Zoe. They're your parents, after all." Harrison tilted her face towards his with his finger. "I've got some money too. I'll be happy to help as much as I can."

Tears stung Zoe's eyes. "You'd really do that for my parents?"

"We're going to be family, soon, so yes." He ran his fingers lightly through her hair as he gazed into her eyes. "That's what families are for."

Smiling, Zoe wiped her eyes as waves of warmth washed through her. "I don't know what to say, Harrison. All those years when you wouldn't even speak to your parents, and now you're happy to help mine?"

"I was young and selfish back then. I now know that family is the only thing that really matters."

She smiled into his soft, brown eyes, her heart overflowing with love. "Thank you." She leaned forward and kissed him slowly. As she pulled back from their kiss, she lifted her hand and stroked his cheek. "I love you, Harrison."

"And I love you too, Zoe." As he lowered his face and continued kissing her, caressing her, for just a moment, Zoe forgot all about the problems her parents were having.

Chapter Four

Zoe tried to push away Mum's words, but they'd entwined themselves in her mind and she couldn't shake them off. As she lay in bed in the dark with the fan whirring and wobbling above her, a mixture of anxiety and anger over her parents' situation wove together tightly in her heart and she didn't know where one ended and the other started. Her temples throbbed and her heart ached.

Just before dawn, she gave up trying to sleep and slipped out of bed and dressed in a clean pair of denim shorts and a lightweight shirt.

Opening her door quietly, Zoe tip-toed down the hallway towards the kitchen. Despite her care, the old floorboards creaked, and she feared she might wake everyone. Entering the kitchen, Zoe pulled up short—Mum sat at the table with her head in her arms. In front of her a Bible lay open.

Zoe inched backwards, but a floorboard creaked and Mum looked up. Her cheeks were damp, and her eyes a watery red. "I'm sorry, Mum," Zoe whispered.

"It's okay, sweetheart. Come and sit down." Mum extended her hand and motioned for Zoe to join her. "How did you sleep?"

"Not well. I couldn't stop worrying about you and Dad—my head was spinning all night."

"I've hardly been sleeping either." Mum let out a sigh.

"I've been trying not to worry, and although I know God will look after us, I have to keep reminding myself of that because it's so easy to start getting anxious."

"Harrison and I were talking last night, Mum, and we want to help. We've got some money saved. It won't be enough, but it'll help."

Mum squeezed Zoe's hand as tears rolled down her cheeks. "Zoe, sweetheart, I appreciate your kindness, but you and Harrison have got your own lives to be planning for. You'll need your money, especially as we won't be able to pay for your wedding." Mum blinked back tears. "I'm so sorry, Zoe. We should be helping you, not the other way around."

"It doesn't matter, Mum. We'll have a simple wedding. And you know what?"

Mum shook her head.

"I think we'll have it here."

Mum raised her brow, an amused look on her face. "You'll have to get married in the next few weeks, then, unless God performs a miracle."

Zoe lifted her chin. "The bank's not going to turn you out, Mum. I won't let them."

Mum let out a small chuckle. "I like your determination, Zoe, but all the determination in the world won't change the fact that we don't have any money to make our repayments."

"Stop talking like that, Mum. I think you and Dad have given up, and that's really sad. The farm's your life, your home, you can't just give up without a fight."

"We haven't given up, Zoe, but maybe God has other plans for us."

Zoe's eyebrows narrowed. "Like what?" Why would God want her parents to leave their home?

Mum shrugged and gave a weak smile. "I don't know yet."

"Well, Harrison and I will fight for you. We're not going

to let you lose the farm without trying everything."

Mum drew a breath and dabbed her eyes. "I don't see what you can do, Zoe, but if you want to try, I guess we can't stop you." She smiled through her tears. "Thanks, Zoe. And I'm so sorry. This should be a happy time for you."

"It's okay Mum." Standing, Zoe squeezed Mum's shoulders and gazed outside at the hills in the distance as ideas for how she and Harrison could save the farm took root in her mind. Mum might be prepared to sit back and wait for God to bail them out, but she certainly wasn't.

Shortly after, Zoe made coffee for both her and Mum and then stepped outside with a mug in her hand. Early morning sunshine streamed through the trees in the distance, splitting the light into a kaleidoscope of colour that shone over the orchard. In the early morning light, it was almost impossible to believe the trees were dying from lack of water.

Zoe paused and admired the beauty of the morning, her worries momentarily forgotten. A movement from the orchard caught her eye. Peter was heading her way, but he hadn't seen her. How would he cope if the farm was lost? Simple answer— he wouldn't. Zoe's heart went out to her kind and loving younger brother whose disability only served to make him more lovable.

"Hey Peter, what are you doing?" Zoe waved him over.

"Just checking the trees. They're dying, Zoe. It's very sad."

Zoe gave him a hug. "I know it is, Peter. But we'll try to save them."

His innocent brown eyes lit up. "Really? You're going to save the trees?"

Zoe gulped. Maybe she shouldn't have said anything. Peter would now be expecting her to do just that—there was no way he'd forget. "We're going to try, Peter, I can't promise, but we'll try. Okay?"

"Okay. Zoe's going to save the trees." He grabbed her hand. "Come and look at my house, Zoe." He dragged her towards the one bedroom flat attached to the side of the main house which Dad and Peter had built recently to give him a little independence. Every time Zoe came to visit, Peter dragged her inside. He was so proud of it. A lump formed in Zoe's throat. Just another reason to save the farm.

"Wipe your feet before you come in, Zoe. Thank you." Peter held the door open for her. "Welcome, Zoe."

"Thank you, Peter. It's very tidy." Peter's little house was always tidy. Nothing was ever out of place, ever.

"Yes, tidy is good. Can I make you a drink?"

"I've already got one, Peter, but thank you."

"Would you like to sit down?"

"Okay." Zoe pulled out a chair from under the small table and sat. Sitting across from her, Peter immediately turned on his laptop computer.

Zoe hooked her feet around the chair legs, and leaning forward, folded her arms on the table. "So what have you been doing, Peter?"

"Playing chess."

"On your computer?"

Peter nodded, a proud grin growing on his face. "I'm good at it, Zoe. I always win."

"You're very clever, Peter."

"I know." His face grew serious. "The trees are sick, Zoe. We need to make them better."

"We're going to try, Peter." Zoe forced a smile but a heavy lump sat in her stomach. How would Peter cope if she failed? She straightened. No time to waste—a plan had to be formulated, and quickly. "I need to get back, Peter. Harrison will be looking for me."

"Harrison's nice, Zoe. I like him."

"I like him too, Peter."

"You love him, Zoe. If you're getting married, you have to love him."

Zoe laughed again. "Yes, you're right, Peter, I love him, and now I need to get back to him."

"Okay. Thanks for visiting, Zoe."

"It's been a pleasure, Peter."

Zoe's chair scraped against the tiled floor as she pushed it back.

Peter covered his ears, his body tensing.

Zoe berated herself—Peter didn't like noise. Reaching out her arm, she placed it lightly on his shoulders. "I'm sorry, Peter, I didn't mean to do that."

He lowered his hands. "It's okay, Zoe. Are you coming to church this morning?"

Zoe chuckled. She was always surprised at what came out of Peter's mouth, but to be honest, she'd forgotten it was Sunday. "I'm not sure, Peter. I'll have to check with Harrison."

"He can come too. He can sit beside me."

Zoe smiled. "He'd like that, Peter. I'll ask him."

"Okay. See you there, Zoe." He ushered her out the door.

"Bye, Peter. See you soon." Zoe gave a cheerful wave, but when she turned away the smile slipped from her face. She blinked as she looked around. Could she really save the farm and the trees?

Harrison was in the kitchen talking with Mum when Zoe entered through the back door. Draping her hand across his shoulder, Zoe leaned down and kissed his cheek. "Sleep well?"

Covering her hand with his, he looked up. As his deep brown eyes met hers, Zoe's heart skipped a beat. It was so easy to lose herself in those eyes of his.

A small grin lifted the corner of his mouth. "Not bad.

And you?"

She knew what he was thinking...he would have slept better if she'd agreed to share his bed. She let out a small sigh. Would he ever accept her decision? Besides, Mum and Dad would never approve.

Straightening, Zoe ran her hand over her hair and tightened her pony tail. "Not so good. Too many things on my mind."

Mum pushed her chair back and picked up the coffee pot from the kitchen counter. "Another coffee, Zoe? I've just made a fresh pot."

"Love one, thanks Mum." Zoe sat beside Harrison and slipped her hand onto his leg. "I met Peter outside." Turning her head, she met Harrison's gaze. "He wants us to go to church."

Harrison's brows shot up.

"He said you could sit beside him."

"But we went on Christmas Day, Zoe. That would make it twice in one week..."

Zoe angled her head. "Is that a problem?"

Harrison blew out a breath. "Guess not."

Soon after, Zoe, Harrison, Ruth, Peter and Grandma stood in the shade of the large Poinciana tree waiting for Dad to join them. Zoe fanned her face to generate some breeze. Maybe she was getting soft, but she couldn't recall ever being so hot.

"Can I go in your car, Harrison?" Peter stood a little too close.

"Sure." Harrison flashed Zoe a 'please help me' type of look, but she just laughed and placed her hand on his shoulder.

"I'll go with Mum and Dad and Grandma."

"Let's go, Harrison." Peter grabbed Harrison's arm and led him towards the sports car parked in the entrance of the big shed.

Zoe chuckled and waved as Harrison glanced back. Harrison was Peter's new best friend whether he liked it or not.

Dad soon appeared, and linking her arm through Grandma's, Zoe walked beside her to the car and helped her into the front seat before hopping into the back with Mum.

A cloud of dust hung over the long gravel driveway. Zoe raised her brow. Harrison had to be driving fast to kick up that much. Peter no doubt was egging him on.

Grandma turned in her seat, a warm smile on her wrinkly face. "This is nice, all going to church together."

Smiling, Zoe nodded. "Yes it is, Grandma." And it was. She leaned back in her seat and gazed out the window as memories came to her of Sunday mornings sitting in the back of the car on the way to church with Peter trying to pull her ribbons out. Where had all the years gone? And why hadn't she kept going when she moved to the city?

Zoe straightened as they approached the small traditional church sitting on top of a hill on the outskirts of town. A narrow band of green grass sat out front, but other than that, the grounds were dry just like everywhere else in town. A number of cars were already parked—Harrison's sports car looked very out of place amongst the large SUV's.

Out of the corner of her eye, a familiar face caught Zoe's attention. Spiky blond hair, with eyes as blue as the sky and framed by long lashes all the girls were prepared to die for, there was no doubt it was Spencer Coleman, her ex-boyfriend. *But what is he doing here?* Last Zoe had heard, he was flying high as a pilot based somewhere overseas.

Chapter Five

As Zoe helped Grandma out of the car, both Spencer and Harrison walked towards her. No doubt Peter would also have seen Spencer and told Harrison he used to be her boyfriend. But what did that matter? It was years ago, and they'd both moved on… well she thought they had. But nevertheless, her legs had gone to jelly at the sight of him.

"Thank you, Zoe. You're such a kind girl." Grandma patted Zoe's hand as she linked her arm through Zoe's.

Zoe smiled. Just as well Grandma was acting as a buffer. Those blue eyes were getting closer. Zoe's heart thudded so loudly Grandma would have to hear it.

"Hey, Zoe!" Spencer lifted his hand in a wave as he strode towards her.

Zoe feigned surprise. "Spencer! I didn't expect to see you here." She leaned in for a kiss, but Harrison's raised eyebrows made her wish she hadn't.

Shoving his hands into the pockets of his bleached cut-off chinos, Spencer looked way too cool for her liking. "I'm working for the Royal Flying Doctor Service. Just home for Christmas. And you?" A familiar smile grew on his face and did strange things to her insides. She forced herself to stay focused. She had to. Harrison and Peter were only a step away.

"The same. Just home for Christmas." She extended her other arm to Harrison, slipping it around his waist. "Spencer, this is Harrison, my fiancé." She lifted her face and met

Harrison's gaze, wincing at his tight expression. "Harrison, this is Spencer, an old friend of mine."

They shook hands, but Harrison's body had tensed, and Spencer's eyebrows lifted. Zoe's shoulders sagged. Harrison had no reason to be jealous, but she could understand that he might feel a little threatened by Spencer's ease of manner.

Grandma let go her hold on Zoe's arm. "I'll leave you young people to get on."

"Oh, Grandma, it's okay. Church is about to start now anyway. We'll walk you in."

"I'll catch you later, Zoe." Spencer flashed another of his all too familiar smiles. He held out his hand to Harrison again. "Nice to meet you, Harrison."

Zoe sucked in a breath and placed her hand over Grandma's. *Men.*

Harrison cupped her elbow and guided her into the small chapel, choosing a pew on the opposite side to where Spencer was now kneeling with his family. Mum, Dad and Peter followed them in. Mum raised an eyebrow before she and Dad knelt and bowed their heads in prayer. This obviously wasn't where they normally sat. Zoe was tempted to kneel as well but decided against it. Harrison would be feeling uncomfortable enough as it was just being in church since he'd stopped going when he stopped talking to his parents when he was a teenager. Grandma just bowed her head beside Zoe, so Zoe followed suit but let out a sigh as she did.

This wasn't how it was supposed to be. She'd been looking forward to being in church again, but now? Why did Spencer have to turn up and spoil everything? And how childish Harrison was being... She slumped back against the pew and fanned herself.

Grandma raised her head and patted Zoe's leg. "Are you okay, Zoe?" Grandma's whispered voice was as sweet as the perfume of the roses that grew in front of her cottage.

29

Zoe lowered her head and gently squeezed Grandma's hand. "Yes, I'm okay. Thanks Grandma."

The organ music grew louder and everyone stood. Zoe helped Grandma to stand and kept hold of her thin arm.

Standing beside Zoe, Harrison held her other hand a little too tightly.

The congregation began singing *"My Hope is Built on Nothing Less"*, a hymn Zoe could still sing without looking at the Hymnal Harrison held in front of her. She looked at it anyway.

As she sang, Zoe's gaze moved slowly around the congregation. So many familiar faces, although the numbers had fallen since she'd last been. Not surprising—many would be visiting family at this time of the year, but several families had left town altogether, Mr. and Mrs. Sullivan amongst them. They'd boarded up the Haberdashery store one day and were gone the next, according to Mum. And then there was the Collins' family. Mr. Collins had a fatal tractor accident a year ago, although there was speculation it wasn't an accident after all. Mrs. Collins sold the farm and moved with the four children back to her family in Melbourne.

But others were still here, including the Coleman family. Zoe was surprised at how much Mr. and Mrs. Coleman had aged. They'd always been youthful looking, but Mr. Coleman's hair was now fully grey, and Mrs. Coleman's arms sagged like an old lady's. But then Zoe's gaze shifted to Spencer and she had a job keeping her heart in check. He'd been her first love, and clearly her heart hadn't forgotten, but nothing good would come of allowing her mind to wander. She pulled it into check and faced the front. The hymn was just finishing, and the words lingered in her mind... *"On Christ the solid rock I stand, all other ground is sinking sand, all other ground is sinking sand."*

Once seated again, Zoe leaned in closer to Harrison despite the heat. She couldn't believe they still hadn't air-conditioned the place. Just two old pedestal fans stirred the hot air around.

Squeezing her shoulder, Harrison kissed the top of her head. Not quite appropriate for a conservative church such as this, but what could she do? And what would the people sitting behind think? Zoe drew in a breath. It didn't matter. Of more importance was what the priest was saying. Zoe sat forward. *The priest was so young!* Amazing! Never would Zoe have expected these country folk to have welcomed such a young, probably inexperienced priest into their church. Maybe they had no choice. But his smile stretched from ear to ear, and his voice was warm and friendly, unlike the old priest who was so formal and boring.

As the priest led the congregation in a Common Prayer, Zoe's heart quickened. It was all so familiar. Deciding to kneel this time, she was surprised when Harrison knelt beside her and followed along, albeit quietly. *'Come, let us worship and bow down, and kneel before the Lord our Maker, For He is our God; we are the people of his pasture and the sheep of his hand. Glory to the Father and to the Son and to the Holy Spirit; as it was in the beginning is now and shall be for ever. Amen.'*

"Amen," Zoe remained kneeling for a moment before retaking her seat. She squeezed Harrison's hand and leaned closer. How much stronger their relationship would be if they both shared a common faith. Was it too much to hope for? Until just the other day, it hadn't been important, in fact, they'd rarely discussed their beliefs even though they'd both grown up in Christian families. But something had been stirring in her spirit since being in church on Christmas Day, and now she was thinking it'd be nice if they were on the same page. If only they'd talked about it before…

The service continued, and Zoe listened with interest to the sermon. By the sound of it, the young priest understood his congregation. "Don't ever give up hope. In 2nd Corinthians 4, verses 16 to 18, we read, '*So we do not lose heart. Though our outer self is wasting away, our inner self is being renewed day by day. For this light momentary affliction is preparing for us an eternal weight of glory beyond all comparison, as we look not to the things that are seen but to the things that are unseen. For the things that are seen are transient, but the things that are unseen are eternal.*'" He looked up and paused, his gaze moving around the congregation. Zoe shifted in her seat.

The priest continued. "As God's precious children, our inheritance is waiting for us in heaven." He paused again. "Some of you are wondering how much longer you can endure here on earth while you wait for that inheritance, and I'm sure you're wondering what good it is if you can't get it now when you need it." He gave an understanding smile. "God knows what we need and He loves us. He'll provide for us in His own time and in His own way. He's promised that He won't let anything happen to us that He won't give us the ability to endure. I know sometimes we question that, but our perception of what we need is different from God's. I encourage you all to submit yourselves to God's sovereign purposes, and in all situations, regardless of how difficult they might seem, pray, 'Your will, Your way, Your time.' Trust Him to give you the inner strength to not just endure your struggles here on earth, but to overcome them and to rejoice in them. We're in God's school, ladies and gentlemen, boys and girls, and Jesus is our teacher. Grow and learn, and welcome challenges as opportunities to become more like Him. God bless you all as you seek to live for Him. Amen."

Zoe sat in silence as she processed the message. Of late, she'd been so distracted with her study and work and life she'd neglected her faith, but not that long ago, it had been real. *God had been real.* What had happened? The truth was that her eyes had been so firmly fixed on the here and now, and on being strong in herself, that she'd walked away from Him. She hadn't needed Him, but there'd always been that little spot deep inside her that knew she did. Maybe Mum was right and God would look after them. Zoe gulped.

The Priest cleared his voice. "Please join me in The Lord's Prayer."

The congregation knelt. As Zoe prayed the familiar prayer, her heart quickened and the words became her prayer. *"Our Father which art in heaven, Hallowed be thy name. Thy kingdom come, Thy will be done in earth, as it is in heaven. Give us this day our daily bread. And forgive us our debts, as we forgive our debtors. And lead us not into temptation, but deliver us from evil: For thine is the kingdom, and the power, and the glory, for ever. Amen."*

Zoe's eyes moistened. *Dear God, I'm sorry. You know I love You. Please forgive me for wandering, and please take me back into Your fold. Forgive me, dear Lord. Thank you.*

As she sat back on her seat, Grandma leaned closer and whispered in Zoe's ear, "Welcome back, Zoe."

Zoe turned her head and smiled through her tears. Grandma's faith was so genuine and real, and her kind words meant so much. A lump caught in Zoe's throat as she dabbed her eyes.

Harrison's eyebrows drew together as he leaned his face close to her cheek. "You're not getting all religious, are you, Zoe?" His voice was soft, but his words swept her fuzzy warmth away in an instant.

Turning her head, she met his deep brown eyes. What could she say? She gave him a warm smile, hoping he'd understand. "No, but I want to live my life with God in it."

He narrowed his eyes. "Sounds like religion to me."

Zoe's heart crumbled. The dream of sharing a common faith was disappearing fast. "Surely you understand?"

"We'll talk about it later."

Placing his hand in the small of her back, Harrison walked beside her out of the chapel and steered her through the crowd. A smile was planted on his face, but Zoe knew it was forced. *God, what's his problem?*

"Leaving so soon, Zoe?"

Zoe stiffened. The one person she could do without seeing at the moment stood in front of them. "Ah…no. We were just getting a drink."

"Let me get you one. Coffee?"

Zoe glanced at Harrison. His smile had slipped. "Thanks, Spencer, but I'll just have water."

"Harrison?"

"I can get my own, thanks anyway." He sounded cordial enough, but there was a crisp edge to his voice.

"Right." Spencer flashed him a puzzled look before stepping towards the drinks' counter and picking up two cups of water and handing one to Zoe.

Harrison didn't move.

"A sip?" Zoe lifted her cup.

Harrison shook his head. "I'm all right, thanks."

"So what do you do, Harrison?" Spencer stood with his feet apart, one hand in the pocket of his chinos. Zoe couldn't help her heart skipping a beat. So relaxed, unlike Harrison who was as taut as the strings on a violin.

"I'm an animal surgeon."

"A vet?" Spencer angled his head.

Harrison bristled. "I'm a specialist surgeon."

"Right." Spencer shifted his attention to Zoe. "Maybe we could all catch up sometime?"

Zoe forced a smile. *Really? Are you just trying to make things worse?* "We'll see." She sipped her water. "Anyway, we must go. Things to do, you know how it is." A shaky laugh bubbled from her throat. "Good to see you, Spencer."

"And you, Zoe." He leaned in and kissed her cheek before extending his hand to Harrison.

"What was that all about, Zoe?" Harrison asked after

they'd told her parents they were going back.

"I don't know what you mean," she replied lightly.

Harrison turned his face and raised a brow. "Yes you do."

"We're just old friends, Harrison, that's all."

"A bit too friendly for my liking."

"Harrison, stop it, will you? Anyone would think you were jealous."

"Is there a reason to be?"

"No." Zoe drew her eyebrows together.

"So what's the story, then?" Harrison kept one eye on the road while shooting Zoe a side-wise glance.

Zoe sighed. He wasn't going to let up. "We went out for a few years in high-school, that's all."

"A few years? That's a long time, Zoe. Seems like he's still keen on you."

Zoe straightened. "No he's not! He dumped me for my best friend!"

Harrison raised an eyebrow. "So where is she now?"

Good question. Zoe shrugged. "Not sure."

"So what does lover-boy do?"

Zoe's head snapped up. "He's not 'lover-boy'." Folding her arms, she narrowed her eyes and studied Harrison's profile. "I don't know what's gotten into you, Harrison. There's nothing between us anymore. Hasn't been for a long time."

Silence hung heavily between them before Harrison released a breath. "I'm sorry, Zoe. I'm not sure what's gotten into me either. Guess I just don't belong out here."

"What are you talking about? Everyone loves you."

He shrugged. As he slowed the car to turn into the driveway, he stretched out his arm, and pulling her close, kissed her cheek. "I'd be happier if you'd marry me sooner than next year."

Their eyes locked. The first traces of doubt niggled her

35

insides, making her feel uncomfortable. She'd promised to marry Harrison, so why was she delaying? Shouldn't she be eager to set a date? They loved each other, wasn't that enough? As she held Harrison's gaze, the words Grandma had spoken to her many years ago floated through her mind. *"Choose wisely, Zoe. Choosing a life partner is the biggest decision you'll make outside of choosing to accept Jesus as Saviour. Make sure the one you choose loves God more than he loves you. Make sure he's a person of good character and is kind to others. Make sure he treats his parents with honour and respect, and that he's respected by others. Understand his priorities. Does he put God first? Does he live to serve others? Is he selfish? Does he anger easily? Ask the Lord for discernment, Zoe. Seek His will and He'll direct your paths. Choose wisely, my dear girl."* She'd pulled Zoe close and kissed the top of her head and then prayed for her. Zoe gulped. Why hadn't she heeded Grandma's advice? Maybe she'd acted too quickly in accepting Harrison's proposal. Did she really know his heart? Maybe deep down he did believe, so who was she to judge? But had she made a mistake? The thought made her ill and her heart heavy. "We need to talk, Harrison."

Harrison's face blanched. "What's wrong, Zoe?"

"We just need to talk, that's all."

"Okay, let's talk. Where do you want to go?"

Zoe swallowed hard. Was she ready for this? She drew a deep breath. "Take a left at the top of the hill and head down to the grove. I'll let Mum know we'll be late for lunch." Zoe pulled out her phone and sent a text. Her hands shook. This could end well, but there was every chance it would end badly. But it had to be done. How could she marry Harrison if she held any doubts?

Chapter Six

Zoe directed Harrison to a group of large gum trees hugging a dry creek bed. She opened her car door, but remained in her seat. Harrison left his door shut, but flicked the switch to open the roof.

An awkward silence sat between them. Harrison rested his elbow on the window frame, his fingers twiddling the steering wheel. He turned his head. "So what do you want to talk about?"

Zoe drew a slow breath. *Lord, please help me say what I need to.* Shifting in her seat, she raised her face and met his gaze. Lifting her hand, she ran the back of her fingers lightly down his cheek. "Harrison, I really do love you, so please take this the right way." She swallowed hard again. His expression tightened…he was expecting her to break their engagement. If she was really heeding Grandma's words, she would. But she couldn't, not yet. "I'm sorry, Harrison, I think I've already said the wrong thing." She gulped. "I'm not breaking it off." Grandma's words rang in her ears.

As she held his gaze, she willed the butterflies in her stomach to calm. "I just need to let you know how I'm feeling, that's all."

Harrison's gaze didn't flinch.

Lowering her hand, she tucked her leg beneath her and

clasped her hands together. "Interrupt me whenever you want."

She inhaled slowly. "I want to marry you, Harrison, but things have changed."

He angled his head, narrowing his eyes. "What things?"

"It started on Christmas Day when we went to church. It was like God was knocking on my heart reminding me He was still there." She paused, remembering how the worship music at Harrison's parents' church had almost made her cry. "I gave my heart to God when I was young. I used to love going to church and learning all about Him." She smiled. "I used to know all the memory verses at Sunday School, in fact, I used to win all the prizes. I was confirmed when I was twelve, and as a teenager, I read the Bible from cover to cover. My faith was real. But I slowly back-slid after I moved to the city and started Uni. I think I missed my friends, and I just got too involved in my study, but going to church on Christmas Day with your family made me start thinking about God again. And then this morning in Church, He touched me for real."

Harrison turned in his seat and folded his arms. "I'm not sure what to say to all that, Zoe. You know I've never really been into all this church stuff."

"But you believe, don't you?"

Harrison raised a brow. "What makes you think that?"

"I watched you on Christmas Day in church. I think God was speaking to you, too." She inhaled slowly. "It was you who asked your mum to invite Tessa and Ben to Christmas lunch, wasn't it?"

His eyes flickered. Was she right, and somewhere deep down he believed? She prayed he did.

She took his hand and threaded her fingers between her

own. "Let's not race into getting married, Harrison. We need to be sure, both of us. Let's take time to really get to know each other, and then if we still both agree, we can set a date then."

His expression eased. "And you won't pressure me into becoming religious?"

She gave a shaky laugh. "No." But was she being honest? Would she marry him if he didn't share her faith? She couldn't tell him that. How pompous and presumptuous would that sound? She squeezed his hand. "I promise I won't pressure you." *But I pray that God will work in your heart and draw you to Himself.* She ran her hand down his cheek. "I love you, Harrison."

He lifted his hand and placed it on top of hers. "I can see this is important to you, Zoe. I've never understood it all, and to be honest, God seems irrelevant to me, but because I love you, I'll try to keep an open mind."

Her eyes moistened as hope wrapped itself around her heart. "That's all I can ask for, Harrison." She had to let God do His work, all the while knowing that the final decision would be Harrison's. He'd either respond to God or he wouldn't.

Leaning forward, he framed her face with his hands and kissed her, tenderly to begin with, but becoming more urgent with every moment, as if he was testing her resolve.

As Zoe finally pulled away, she looked deep into his softened eyes and her heart almost broke. Would she ever be able to break it off with him if she was faced with the decision of being obedient to God or going her own way and marrying a non-believer? If only she'd heeded Grandma's words before they fell in love…

Harrison tipped her chin, a glint in his eye. "So we've

got that sorted. What's next?"

Zoe straightened her shirt and blew out a breath. Her heart was still racing, and she felt hot and clammy. "Let's go for a walk."

He smiled at her. "Good idea."

They climbed out of the car and Harrison took her hand as they strolled along under the lemon scented gum trees. Normally the grass was green and soft, but with the drought conditions so severe, even here the grass, what was left of it, was so dry it crunched under foot. But this was where she wanted to be married. *If they got married.*

They weaved through the trees and played hide and seek amongst the trees just like she did as a kid.

Zoe melted into his arms when he grabbed her from behind. She laughed as he turned her around and popped a kiss on her lips. "I haven't had this much fun in a long time, Harrison."

"Me either." A grin split his face as he lowered his lips against hers.

"Guess we'd better get back." Reluctantly, Zoe released herself from his arms. She could have stayed there all day.

Nodding, Harrison ran his hand lightly down her cheek before taking her hand and leading her back to the car.

Back in her seat, Zoe noticed the flashing light on her phone. Picking it up, her chest tightened. *Ten missed calls from Mum.* "Something's happened, I just know it." She quickly dialled Mum's number and kept her eyes on Harrison, all the while trying to remain calm, but inside, her stomach churned.

Mum answered within three rings.

"Zoe, I've been trying to call you. Grandma's collapsed and she's having trouble breathing."

Zoe clutched the phone with both hands. *Not Grandma...* "Where is she?"

"At her cottage. We were just dropping her off."

"We'll be there right away." Zoe hung up and gave Harrison directions. "Continue straight, and then turn right just before the top."

He hit the accelerator. The tyres spun in the dirt, causing a cloud of dust to billow behind them as they climbed the dirt track to the top of the hill.

Zoe forced herself to breathe slowly and to think. It would most likely be Grandma's heart. She should call an ambulance, but what were the chances of getting one out here quickly enough?

"That's her cottage up there." Zoe pointed to the small white cottage in the distance where Grandma had lived on her own since Grandfather's death just over five years ago. She liked her independence, but they all worried about her.

Harrison brought the car to a stop beside Dad's SUV and Zoe jumped out, not even bothering to wait for the dust to settle. She took the stairs two at a time and raced inside.

Mum appeared from Grandma's room, her face pale and her eyes heavy with worry. "Zoe, I'm so glad you're here. Grandma's on her bed. Come quickly."

Zoe pushed past Mum and entered Grandma's room. The scent of lavender filled her nostrils, invoking so many fond memories, but this wasn't the time for a trip down memory lane. Zoe slowed as she stepped closer. It was almost impossible to see Grandma in the large four poster bed, but the wheezing coming from the bed left Zoe in no doubt Grandma lay there amongst the bed covers and cushions. Sitting beside her on a chair, Zoe reached for Grandma's hand and felt for a pulse. Grandma's eyes fluttered, pain written all over them.

"Where does it hurt, Grandma?" Leaning forward, Zoe gently stroked her forehead.

Grandma lifted her hand slowly and placed it on her chest. Zoe had guessed correctly... Grandma was having a heart attack.

"We need to sit you up, Grandma. Dad, can you help?" Zoe waited while Dad scooted around the other side of the bed. Together, they lifted her gently. Zoe tucked several pillows behind her back and one under her legs.

"Mum, do you know where her medication is?"

"Yes, I'll go grab it." Mum disappeared in a flurry and returned almost immediately with a bottle of Nitroglycerin. Zoe took the bottle and took one tablet out and placed it under Grandma's tongue.

"We need to get her to hospital as quickly as possible." Zoe looked first at Dad and then at Mum.

"We'll need to drive her ourselves, Zoe." Dad's voice sounded strained. "We called for an ambulance, but it'll be two hours before it gets here. Dr. Johnson's on leave, and the on-call doctor's out already. We have no choice."

"What about the Flying Doctor Service? Surely they'd come?" As soon as she said it, an idea sprang into her head. "Wait, I've got an idea. Spencer has a plane. I'll call him." Harrison may not like it, but she didn't care. Getting Grandma to hospital as quickly as possible was her only concern right now, and it'd be quicker than waiting for the Flying Doctor to come.

"Do you have the Colemans' phone number, Mum?"

Mum fumbled with her phone. "I think so, but here, you do it, Zoe." She handed the phone to Zoe.

Taking it from her, Zoe scrolled quickly to 'C' and found the number. She hit the green call icon and prayed they'd pick up.

After four rings, Mrs. Coleman's voice sounded on the other end, a voice Zoe hadn't heard for some time. "Hello, Doris Coleman speaking."

"Mrs. Coleman, this is Zoe Taylor. Is Spencer available?" No time for chit-chat.

"Ah, yes... I'll just get him." Mrs. Coleman sounded a little put out.

Zoe drew a breath. All eyes were on her, including Harrison's.

"Zoe, I didn't expect to hear from you so soon."

"It's not a social call, Spencer. I need to ask you a favour."

"Go on."

"Do you have a plane you can use?" She held Dad's gaze while she waited for Spencer's reply.

"Yes..." Spencer sounded puzzled. "What's up?"

"Grandma's had a heart attack, a bad one, and we need to get her to hospital." Zoe gulped. What she was about to ask was very presumptuous. "I was hoping you could take her."

Silence. She could just imagine what he was thinking. After several seconds of waiting, he finally replied. "Sure. It's not the medical plane, just an old farm plane, only licensed to carry three people, but it'll do the job. Can you get her here?"

Zoe nodded eagerly, even though Spencer couldn't see her. "Yes, we'll be there in ten minutes."

"I'll be ready and waiting."

Zoe let out a relieved breath. "Thanks Spencer." She hung up and quickly updated Mum and Dad. "We'll need to carry her carefully into your car, Dad. Mum, can you pack a few of her things?" Turning to Harrison, she rubbed his arm. The frosty look had left his face and he almost looked eager to help. "Can you get Dad's car ready?"

He nodded, and she gave him a grateful smile.

Everyone busied themselves with their jobs. Zoe helped Dad lift Grandma carefully off the bed and into his arms. Being so light, it wasn't difficult at all. Harrison had the car ready and waiting with the engine running. Zoe helped Dad place her gently onto the back seat and asked Mum to grab a pillow.

Zoe slipped in beside her while Dad got in the front. She grabbed the pillow off Mum and placed it behind Grandma's head. In that instant, Zoe's heart went out to Mum. Whilst Grandma was special to Zoe, she was even more special to Mum, and there was a very real possibility they may lose her. "Mum, sit in the back with us. Peter can go with Harrison."

A look of relief flowed over Mum's face. Climbing into the back seat, she sat on the other side of Grandma and took Grandma's frail hand in hers.

Dad reversed the car away from the cottage and then took off down the gravel road toward the Coleman's farm.

Zoe kept watch over Grandma. Her breathing grew more difficult with each passing minute. Rubbing Grandma's hand gently, Zoe fought the tears lurking behind her eyes. "Come on, Grandma, hang in there. Stay with us, please." Fear of losing her clutched Zoe's stomach. Would they get Grandma to the hospital in time? If only there was one closer which could deal with medical emergencies like this. They'd have to fly her to the city where she'd have the best chance of survival. But would they get her there in time?

Dad slowed as he turned into the Colemans' driveway.

Zoe glanced out the window. In the distance to the left, a small single engine plane sat on the farm's makeshift runway, a grass paddock with orange cones as markers. Spencer lifted his hand in a wave as they approached.

Dad parked the car beside the plane and jumped out, shaking Spencer's hand quickly before opening the back door of the car.

Harrison and Peter pulled up beside Dad's car and climbed out.

Dad and Spencer lifted Grandma out of the car and carried her to the plane.

As Zoe went to follow, Harrison caught her hand. "What's the plan, Zoe?"

She gulped. She should have involved him more rather than making him feel like an appendage, but at least he didn't sound too put out.

"I need to go with her, Harrison. You understand, don't you?"

He was struggling, no two ways about it. She guessed she'd struggle, too, if he was about to fly off with an old flame and leave her behind. "I guess so, but I'm not overly happy about it."

"Thank you. I'll be back as soon as I can. I love you." She stretched up and placed a kiss on his lips before pulling her hand away and running to the plane.

Spencer had positioned Grandma on one of the two back seats and was making her as comfortable as possible with the cushions they'd brought along with them.

"I hope she'll be comfortable enough, Zoe." Spencer's nearness and his warm smile caused an unexpected tremor to run through her body. Zoe chided herself—that reaction was most inappropriate.

Crouching in front of her, Zoe wiped Grandma's brow with a damp cloth and repositioned the cushions. Grandma's eyes fluttered and her mouth opened as if she wanted to say something, but she was so breathless she couldn't get any words out.

"It's okay, Grandma, just rest."

Dad stood on the step with one hand on the door. "We'll be praying, Zoe. Look after her." Dad's eyes glistened as he leaned forward and squeezed Grandma's hand. "You're in good hands, Esme." His voice caught. Stepping back, he closed the door.

Spencer climbed into the front seat, did his seat belt up and adjusted the controls before turning his head to the back. Blue eyes twinkled at her. "Strap yourself in, Zoe, we're just about ready for take-off."

Ordering her heart to behave, Zoe nodded and fastened her belt before double checking Grandma's.

"I'll try to make it as smooth as possible, but this runway's a bit bumpy," Spencer called out as he switched on the ignition.

The noise of the engine made further conversation impossible. Zoe nodded again and gave him a smile before he turned his head to the front.

As the plane began to move, Zoe looked out the tiny window and waved to Mum, Dad, Harrison and Peter. Whilst Mum and Dad had their arms around each other and Peter, Harrison stood alone. She bit her lip. Would they survive this unexpected turn of events?

As the plane bounced along the runway before slowly

lifting, Zoe gripped the sides of the small fold down seat and prayed they'd make it safely into the air.

Spencer turned his head around briefly and grinned as they banked to the left. As their eyes met, Zoe once again ordered her heart to behave. She focused her attention on Grandma instead. Reaching out, Zoe squeezed Grandma's hand. Despite the hot day, her hand was icy. Zoe reached for a light blanket from the locker and placed it over Grandma, tucking it gently around her.

"Better?" Smiling, Zoe brushed some wispy grey hair back off Grandma's face with the tips of her fingers.

Grandma nodded, her lips trembling as she attempted a smile.

A heavy weight settled in Harrison's stomach as the small plane carrying Zoe away from him slowly lifted above the tree line, growing smaller with every passing second. Yes, Zoe's Grandma needed urgent medical attention, but how could he feel comfortable with Zoe flying off with Spencer? He didn't trust the guy. He glanced at his watch. If he left now, he'd be back in Brisbane by early evening.

Standing with Ruth and Kevin, Peter continued waving even when the plane was just a speck in the sky and the sound no more than a hum.

Harrison gulped. He'd been so busy worrying about Zoe flying off with Spencer he hadn't considered how everyone else was feeling. Of course they'd be worried about Grandma. According to Zoe, there was every possibility she may not make it.

"Grandma's sick. Zoe's making her better." Peter's voice was monotone as he rocked on his heels and repeated the phrase for the hundredth time.

"Zoe will do her best, Peter." Kevin squeezed Peter's shoulder and then directed him towards the car. "Time to go now."

"Can I go with Harrison?"

Harrison was caught. He cleared his throat. "Actually, I was thinking I'd drive back to the city." He angled his head. "Would one of you like to come?"

"I'll go with you." Peter's face lit up as he bounced on the spot.

Harrison groaned. *How was he going to get out of this?*

Kevin placed a steadying hand on Peter's shoulder. "No, Peter, we should let Mum go so she can be with Grandma."

"Okay…" Peter hung his head, his bottom lip protruding.

Harrison felt bad—he shouldn't have said anything in front of Peter. "You can drive back with me to the house if you like."

Peter's expression immediately changed. "Can I drive?"

Harrison laughed. "Not this time, I'm sorry."

"That's all right. But can we go fast?"

"Maybe." Harrison ruffled Peter's hair and followed him to the car.

Within half an hour, Harrison and Ruth were on their way back to Brisbane.

Chapter Seven

Several times Zoe tried to talk with Spencer, but the drone of the plane's engine made it almost impossible to hear each other with her sitting in the back, so she settled in for the ride and stroked Grandma's hand, wiping her forehead and checking every few minutes that she was still breathing.

Grandma's eyes fluttered open every now and then, but she mainly just sat there, her chest shuddering as she struggled for breath. As Zoe gazed at the sweet little old lady, she forced back tears while sending up prayers for her, hoping God would answer. She wasn't ready to lose Grandma just yet.

Zoe wiped her eyes and glanced out the window at the wide open spaces below, brown as far as her eyes could see, the only green coming from the occasional groupings of trees and the very rare paddock where some optimistic farmer had planted some crops. Smoke from a number of bush fires drifted upwards in lazy spirals until they petered out, dissipating into the air. Rain, and lots of it, was so badly needed. When would God send it? The sermon that morning came to Zoe's mind. If the priest was correct, God may or may not send it sometime soon, but He would somehow still provide for the people who so desperately needed it. Zoe struggled to understand. Why wouldn't God send rain now when it was so obviously needed? She let out a sigh. *God, please help me to understand Your ways.*

Shifting her gaze back to Grandma, Spencer's shapely arm muscles caught Zoe's attention. Against her better judgment, she allowed her eyes to linger on him, and a whole heap of memories flooded back. She was twelve when the Coleman's bought the property next to theirs. Her parents invited the whole family over for a barbecue to welcome them, and that was when she first lay eyes on Spencer Coleman. She still remembered it as if it were yesterday. It was one of those lazy Sunday afternoons when all the jobs were done and she and Peter were free to do whatever they wanted. The one caveat, she had to look after Peter. That wasn't so hard. She just bribed him with sweets she'd put aside for just that purpose. That afternoon, she and Peter had just come back from swimming in the dam when this big old Landcruiser bounced up the driveway, sending a cloud of brown dust into the blue sky.

The car pulled up outside their house, and out jumped three kids—two girls and a boy. It was the boy who drew Zoe's attention. She'd never seen hair so blond nor eyes so blue. And when he grinned at her… Zoe smiled at the memory, her heart melted.

After the introductions had been made, Zoe knew the name of the boy she'd fallen in love with. *Spencer.* The name rolled off her tongue. She tried not to stare at him. Mum placed a hand on her shoulder, making her jump. "Zoe, why don't you show the children the stables? You could even go for a ride if you like. Dinner won't be for a while."

Zoe couldn't believe her luck, even if the others were with them, it didn't matter. She was going to spend time with *him.*

The butterflies in Zoe's stomach didn't settle the whole afternoon and evening, and she could barely tear her eyes away from him. She kept pinching herself that she, Zoe Taylor, quiet, shy and boring, was in the company of the best looking boy she'd ever met, and that he was actually talking with her, and seemed to find her interesting.

Over the ensuing months and years, she and Spencer became best friends, and then boyfriend and girlfriend. On her sixteenth birthday, Spencer gave her a friendship ring and promised to love her forever. But then, less than a month later, she discovered him kissing Lisa. So much for his promise of love.

Zoe drew a slow breath. The hurt of that betrayal had run deep for many years, but she'd forced herself to move on and had immersed herself initially in the church, and then when she moved to the city, in her studies and with her new friends. But then she met Harrison, and now he'd promised to love her forever. Zoe sighed. Would he keep that promise, or would he, like Spencer, also let her down? What was the glue that held a couple together and made their marriage last the distance?

Grandma's words came flooding back to her. Zoe turned her head and looked at Grandma and smiled. She and Grandfather had been happily married for almost fifty years before he passed away. They knew the secret. They'd chosen wisely and put God first. Zoe's heart tightened. That was the problem…would Harrison decide to put God first, and if he didn't, would she be strong enough to let him go?

Harrison rubbed the back of his neck and glanced at the clock on the dashboard. They'd only been on the road an hour... at least four to go. Beside him, Ruth stared out the window as the miles slipped by. He should be making an effort to talk to his future mother-in-law, but he couldn't get Zoe out of his mind. As much as she'd assured him she had no feelings for Spencer, niggling doubts ate away at him, and all he wanted to do was get there as quickly as possible. The thought of her spending any time alone with Spencer made him anxious. At least she was in the back of the plane, but they'd be landing soon, and here he was, in the middle of nowhere. He let out a frustrated sigh. Nothing he could do about it other than keep driving. He'd call her as soon as they had mobile reception again. How could there still be black holes in the country where phones didn't work? Unbelievable!

"Are you worried about Zoe?" Ruth shifted her gaze from the road and looked at him. Was it that obvious?

Harrison tapped the steering wheel. "About her and Spencer, you mean?"

Ruth nodded.

Harrison took a deep breath. "A little."

"You've got nothing to worry about, Harrison. Zoe loves you."

He gave her an appreciative smile, but did she mean it, or was she just being kind?

As he changed down gears and swung out onto the other side of the road to overtake a slow cattle truck, the control panel of the car beeped and the temperature gauge flashed a warning. Harrison's shoulders slumped. The mechanic said he'd fixed the overheating problem. Sighing, he pulled back in behind the truck and slowed down.

Ruth's eyebrows puckered. "What's the problem?"

"Car's overheating. We'll need to stop and let it cool down. Sorry."

"That's not good, especially out here."

"No, it's not." He let out another sigh as the cattle truck disappeared into the distance. One solitary tree near the edge of the road offered a small amount of shade. Harrison slowed the car right down and parked under it. Turning the air-con off but leaving the engine running, he lifted the bonnet. In this heat, it'd take ages for it to cool down. Taking out his phone, he flipped it open. As expected, no reception. He peered back the way they'd come. Nothing. Not a car, not a truck, not a single building—just a long straight road that stretched as far as the eye could see. He peered the other way. The cattle truck was a mere blot in the distance. He should have flashed his lights and stopped it.

"Think we'll be here for a while, sorry." He put both hands behind his head and leaned against the car.

"It's okay, Harrison, I'm used to it. Somebody will come by soon." Ruth gave him a reassuring smile.

Harrison raised a brow. Who was she kidding? "I'll check the coolant level shortly. I've got a bit of water I can put in."

"We might need that for drinking."

Ruth had a point—they could die out here without water. "How far's the next town?"

"Half an hour?" She tilted her head.

"Right, once it's cooled a little, I'll just use a small amount and then we'll take it slowly."

She patted his shoulder and smiled. "You're in charge."

That was the last thing he felt. He was a city boy,

stranded on a deserted country road. A fish out of water couldn't have felt any less in charge than he did right now. And worse still... Zoe would be landing in Brisbane any time now, *with Spencer*, and it was highly unlikely that he and Ruth would make it back tonight.

Zoe looked out the window as the plane began its descent. Smaller properties replaced the wide open plains, and eventually suburbs with houses butting up against each other, many with swimming pools in their backyards, filled her vision. The river snaked its way to the bay in the distance, but instead of heading towards the main Brisbane airport, Spencer banked to the right and approached the smaller airport to the south west of the city. He'd radioed ahead and had clearance to land. Zoe steeled herself for the landing. It was bad enough in a big plane, but in a little thing like this?

She held her breath as the plane wobbled and bounced, and only released it when the plane taxied towards the waiting ambulance. They'd made it.

The transfer to the ambulance was smooth, and within minutes, Paramedics were attending to Grandma. Zoe filled them in, and was congratulated on her swift action. "Getting her to hospital quickly was the best thing you could have done. We'll have her there within fifteen minutes."

Gently brushing Grandma's wispy grey hair, Zoe leaned forward and kissed her cheek. "You're in good hands, Grandma. I'll be waiting for you at the hospital."

Grandma's lips lifted slightly, and she tried to reach for Zoe's hand.

"Save your energy, Grandma, it's okay." Zoe smiled at her. "I'll be praying for you." Zoe pushed back tears as she uttered another silent prayer.

As the ambulance sped away, Zoe pulled out her phone to call a taxi.

Spencer appeared beside her. "I'll come with you, Zoe. Just let me park the plane."

"That's kind of you, Spencer, but there's no need. You've already done too much."

"It's no problem, Zoe. I'd like to."

Maybe he was trying to make up for the way he'd treated her. He didn't need to...she'd moved on, but as Zoe looked into Spencer's eye, it was just like yesterday, and they were still boyfriend and girlfriend. How easy it'd be to fall into his arms and let him kiss her. Her eyes widened. What was she thinking?

"It really is okay, Spencer. I'll be fine." She forced a smile and told her heart once again to behave.

"I insist. Besides, it'll give us a chance to catch up properly."

What if I don't want to? Zoe raised a brow, but it appeared she had no choice. "Okay, but there's really no need."

She phoned for a taxi, and by the time it arrived, Spencer had parked the plane and had done the necessary paperwork. As they climbed into the back of the taxi, all Zoe could think of was what Harrison would say if he saw her now.

Half an hour later, Harrison carefully eased the cap off the radiator. Steam escaped, but the cap didn't blow. The level wasn't as low as he expected. He poured the water slowly, grateful for having had an old car in his student days that overheated all the time. If he hadn't, he most likely would have poured all the water in at once, possibly cracking the head. Zoe would be impressed he knew that. He smiled to himself. He could just see the look on her face.

"All okay, Harrison?" Ruth stood beside him, arms crossed, a hopeful expression on her face.

"Think so. Fingers crossed we make it to the next town." He replaced the radiator cap and closed the bonnet.

Harrison kept one eye on the temperature gauge as he eased the car back onto the road and inched it towards the next town. The temperature climbed slowly. He crossed his fingers they'd make it without the need to stop again. But would they find a mechanic to look at it on a Sunday afternoon out here? Unlikely.

Almost an hour later, twice as long as it would normally take, a signpost indicated they were entering the township of "Arlington", population fifty-three. Harrison shook his head. Fat chance of finding a mechanic.

As the car crawled into town, his fears were confirmed. Joe's Mechanical Repairs was closed and empty. The only place open was the pub, where a number of cars, mainly pick-ups with an assortment of farm equipment in the back, and big SUV's, were parked out front. None of them looked anything like his tiny sports car. Loud music spilled out of the bar area, and a mangy dog cocked his leg on a pole. Harrison winced. It definitely wasn't a place he'd normally frequent.

He let out a sigh. There was no option. Pulling up beside a white LandCruiser, he flipped open his phone.

"Reception?" Ruth asked.

He nodded. "One bar. I'll call Roadside Assistance."

"Doubt they'll come this far. The mechanic's probably inside."

Harrison closed his phone. Entering a noisy country bar wasn't his activity of choice, but he'd do it. "Okay, I'll go in. Happy to wait here?"

"I'll sit in the shade."

"I'll be as quick as I can."

Harrison took a deep breath before entering the "Arlington Hotel". The old building was in good shape considering its location and age. At least the paint wasn't peeling off, and at first glance, it seemed relatively clean. He stepped inside and peered into the public bar on the right. Three men, all wearing shorts and sleeveless shirts, perched on bar stools, chatting to each other. Each had a drink in one hand and a cigarette in the other. One of them must have just told a joke, as they all let out a raucous laugh at the same time.

Harrison hesitated, not really wanting to intrude, and was about to walk on when one of them called out.

"Come and join us, son. We won't bite." The man was missing a bottom tooth and his skin was so sun wizened it looked like the skin of a crocodile, but his smile seemed genuine.

"Thanks." Harrison stepped towards the group. "But I was really just looking for the mechanic. Is he around?"

"That would be me." The toothless man put his drink down and held out his hand. "Joe Jenkins. What can I do for you?"

Harrison grimaced, but shook the man's hand anyway. "My car's overheating. Harrison's the name."

Raising his eyebrows, Joe chuckled. "Not unusual on a

day like today. It's hot enough to fry an egg in the shade." He stubbed out his cigarette and skulled the remainder of his beer. "Come on then, sonny, let's take a look." He placed a hand on Harrison's shoulder, and walked with him outside.

"Snazzy car."

"Thanks." Right now, it'd be better if it wasn't quite so snazzy.

"Lift the bonnet."

Harrison opened the car door and pulled the lever.

Joe lifted the bonnet and took a quick look. "Needs to cool down before I check it properly, but seems fixable. I can look at it first thing in the morning."

Harrison's shoulders slumped. Not what he wanted to hear. "Any chance you could look at it today?"

"Nuh mate, don't work on Sunday's. You and your missus will have to stay the night, unless you want to risk breaking down in the middle of nowhere."

Harrison laughed. "I don't have a "missus" yet. I'm travelling with my fiancée's mother."

Joe's face crinkled as Ruth joined them. "Ruth! What a sight for sore eyes. Fancy seeing you here."

"Joe! Good to see you too." Smiling, Ruth held out her hand. "How long have you lived here?"

"Goin' on three years. Bought the joint after I left you guys."

Joe wiped his hand on his shorts before taking hers and shaking it. His forehead puckered as he glanced quickly at Harrison. "Where are you off to?"

"Long story…Mum's been flown to Brisbane." Her expression sobered. "Heart attack. Zoe's with her, and Harrison and I are on our way there now."

"Sad to hear that, Ruth. Maybe I can make an exception and get you on the road tonight."

"That'd be wonderful, Joe." Ruth glanced at Harrison. "We'd appreciate that."

"See what I can do. Still need to let it cool down. Might be a few hours."

"That's not a problem, Joe. I'm sure we can fill them in."

"Righteo." He turned to Harrison. "Drive it to my workshop down the road and I'll meet you there."

"Will do." Harrison turned to Ruth. "Would you prefer to come with me or stay here?"

"I'll come." She climbed into the seat beside Harrison.

Harrison reversed the car out onto the road and drove slowly back the way they'd come, stopping in front of Joe's workshop.

Pulling in behind them, Joe hopped out of his pickup and unlocked the rusty gate. "Drive her in, mate. Keep going, that's the way."

As Harrison followed Joe's instructions and squeezed the car inside the workshop, he began to wonder if this was the right place to take his car. It was nothing like the immaculate dealer workshop he normally used, where customers were greeted by a receptionist dressed in a smart uniform, and a complimentary car was offered for the day. No resemblance to this joint at all. Here, the smell of oil and petrol fumes filled the air, and a layer of grime coated everything. Vehicle parts of all shapes and sizes filled the work benches, and there was no room to move.

"Be careful, Ruth, you don't want to get grease on you." Harrison spoke quietly. "I should have let you out before I drove in."

"It's okay, Harrison. I'm used to it. Joe worked for us for years."

"Right." He opened the door, being careful not to open it too wide, and squeezed out between his car and the dirty old truck parked alongside it. If he got grease on his nice new shorts...

Joe threw a cigarette butt on the ground and stubbed it out with his shoe. "I'll give you a lift back to the hotel and I'll come back later and fix it."

"Thanks Joe, that's very kind of you," Ruth said, emerging from her side of the car.

"Pleasure, Ruth. Wouldn't do it for no-one else." Joe chuckled, his smile lighting up with his weather-beaten face.

"Oh come on, Joe, you're a big softy. Everyone knows that."

The banter between the two surprised Harrison, but it was just as well—they'd be staying the night otherwise...a few hours was bad enough.

The inside of Joe's truck was just as dirty as the inside of his workshop. Harrison shrugged and gave up trying to stay clean. Arriving back at the hotel, Joe showed them into the lounge. The air-conditioning was a welcome surprise. Harrison ordered a beer for himself, and a cup of tea for Ruth, and settled in for the afternoon. Definitely not what he'd planned, but it could have been a whole lot worse.

Chapter Eight

Without even looking, Zoe knew exactly who was calling when her phone rang as she sat in the Emergency Department beside Spencer. "I've got to take this, Spencer. I won't be long." She gave him an apologetic smile as she stood and stepped into the corridor. The invisible weight still sat heavily in her stomach and on her heart despite the hundred or more times she'd handed the situation with Harrison over to God. How could she have done this? Promised to marry Harrison one day and regretted it the next? But she loved him, that was the problem. Her heart was torn. Surely God had a solution.

She inhaled slowly before answering.

"Harrison, I was just about to call."

"Zoe, finally… how's your Grandma?" Harrison sounded flustered.

"Still with us, thank God. She's being assessed."

"I'm on my way with your mum. We were hoping to be there soon, but the car broke down and I'm stuck in this little town with your mother for the next few hours while it gets fixed."

Zoe laughed. "You're what?"

"You heard." She imagined him raking his hand through his hair.

"You're lucky it can be fixed on a Sunday."

"I know. Your mum knew the mechanic, that helped a lot."

"How's Mum doing?" She spoke quietly.

"She's doing okay, considering. Zoe…"

"Yes…" Her heart thumped.

"Are you all right?"

"Yes, Spencer's here with me." Zoe hit her head. Why had she said that?

Silence.

"It's okay, Harrison. He's just waiting with me."

"Okay." She could hear the tension in his voice.

"I'll let you know about Grandma as soon as I hear. And Harrison, don't worry about Spencer." She gulped. "I love you."

Her heart thumped while she waited for a reply.

When he did, his voice had softened and held a faint tremor. "I love you too, Zoe. I miss you."

His words wrapped around her heart, sending a wave of warmth through her body, but they didn't solve her problem, in fact, they only made it worse. "Get here as soon as you can, Harrison. And drive carefully."

"I will."

Leaning against the wall after she hung up, Zoe took a few moments before returning to her seat. Maybe a few hours with Mum was God's doing. The thought gave her hope, and once again she prayed God would touch his heart, because the very thought of telling Harrison she couldn't marry him was breaking hers.

Straightening, Zoe walked to the water fountain and poured some chilled water into a paper cup and took a sip, the cool water sliding down her throat, soothing her body and her soul.

Spencer looked up and smiled as she sat beside him, sending her heart back into turmoil. How could one look from those blue eyes do that to her? She bit her lip.

He raised a brow. "All okay?"

She took a deep breath and nodded. "Mum and Harrison are on their way."

"Do you love him, Zoe?" His blue eyes lifted, probing hers, bringing back unwanted memories of when they were young and in love.

Her heart quickened. She needed to put him right, because if she didn't… "Yes, I do." She swallowed hard.

He lowered his eyes and studied his hands. Seconds passed before he looked back up. "I'm sorry for the way I treated you, Zoe."

Her heart began to crumble and once again she was sixteen, seeing her boyfriend kissing her best friend. Tears welled in her eyes. He'd never apologised until now.

"I hurt you, and it was wrong. Will you forgive me?"

Dabbing her eyes, Zoe drew a slow breath. Until this morning, she thought she'd put it behind her, but seeing him again had revived the hurt and pain of betrayal. Maybe she did need to forgive him. She nodded. She didn't trust herself to speak.

Spencer held her gaze. "I hope he loves you, Zoe. He's a lucky man."

She sucked in a breath to steady herself before releasing it. "He does."

"I'm glad." Somehow she knew he meant it.

She lifted her eyes and met his gaze. "And what about you and Lisa?"

Spencer's face clouded. "She wasn't a patch on you, Zo, but that's another story. We're not together anymore."

"And you've come home?"

He nodded, his expression brightening. "Nothing beats being near the family."

"Mum and Dad might lose the farm." Zoe gulped. She hadn't meant to tell him, it just came out.

Spencer's eyes widened. "No!"

Zoe swallowed hard and nodded. She still couldn't believe it herself.

"What happened?"

Zoe blew out a breath and told him everything. Spencer understood—his parents were struggling too, and had almost invested in the same scam.

"I'll help you find the guy, Zoe. I've got contacts."

Zoe's eyes moistened. "Would you?"

"Absolutely. He's not going to get away with this."

She smiled at him as she dabbed her eyes. "Thank you, Spencer."

Just then, a young male doctor with dark black hair pushed the swing doors open and looked around. "Miss Taylor?"

"Over here." Straightening, Zoe lifted her hand and then blew her nose.

The doctor took a seat beside her, his dark eyes serious. "Your Grandma's still critical but stable." He spoke slowly. "She's on medication to thin her blood, but she needs Bypass surgery. We'll schedule her as soon as we can."

Zoe drew a breath. "Will she make it?"

"We're doing our best." His eyes held steady.

"Can I see her?"

"We're moving her into ICU. You can visit her there in about half an hour."

Zoe offered the best smile she could manage. "Thank you."

The doctor nodded as he stood. "We'll do our best, Miss Taylor."

Spencer took her hand as the doctor walked away, rubbing his thumb gently over her skin.

Warmth from his strong hand flowed up her arm and into her heart. She closed her eyes. It should be Harrison sitting here, comforting her, not Spencer. They had too many memories, and it would do her no good to venture down that path any further. She pulled her hand away.

"I'm sorry Spencer. I need to wait on my own." Tears stung her eyes, but she'd made her decision.

"I understand." Spencer stood slowly and gave her a wistful smile. "If ever he lets you down, you know where I am."

She could hardly bear it. But no, she could never fully trust him again, even though she'd forgiven him. She forced a smile. "Thanks for the ride, Spencer."

"My pleasure, Zoe."

Zoe pushed back tears as Spencer disappeared out the door, her heart heavy with the sorrow of lost love. Why was it so hard to do the right thing? But was it right to keep Harrison dangling now that she was having doubts? Her throat clenched. If only she hadn't been so quick to accept his proposal. *God, you've got to work this out. I sure can't.*

She remained in her seat for another ten minutes and prayed for Harrison, beseeching God to draw him to Himself. She loved him, and she couldn't bear the thought of losing him just because he didn't love God. He was a good man. He was kind and thoughtful, he loved his family and he felt remorse about the way he'd treated his parents. He loved animals, he was intelligent and good-looking, he had a sense of humour, and he loved her. But he didn't love God. *Yet.* She blew out a breath.

Standing, Zoe walked outside into the hot, humid air, thinking she'd walked straight into a Swedish Sauna. Wiping her already damp brow with the back of her hand, she remained in the shade of the covered entrance, pulled her phone out and dialled Harrison's number.

He answered on the first ring. "Zoe…"

"He's gone, Harrison. You don't have to worry anymore."

"I wasn't worrying."

"Yes you were."

"Maybe a bit."

"How about a big bit?" Her heart warmed at their banter.

Harrison let out a chuckle. "Okay, you win. I was worried sick."

Zoe laughed. "I knew it. Anyway, he's gone, no need to worry anymore."

"I'm glad." He sounded relieved.

"I need to talk to Mum about Grandma. Is she there?"

"I'll pass you over. I love you, Zoe."

"I love you too." Zoe drew a breath. She could never give him up.

"Zoe…" Mum came on the phone, sounding worried.

"Mum, Grandma's okay—she needs Bypass Surgery, but she's stable at the moment."

Mum let out a relieved sigh. "Thank God you got her there so quickly."

"She wouldn't have made it if we hadn't."

"I've been praying for her." Mum's voice faltered.

"And so have I."

"We'll be there as soon as we can."

"How much longer before you can leave?'

"Still not sure. Hopefully soon."

"Okay, take care. I love you, Mum."

"I love you, too, Zoe."

Zoe wiped tears from her eyes as an ambulance siren wailed in the distance.

Ruth returned the phone to Harrison and leaned back in her chair. The delay had been frustrating, but it had given her time to talk with Harrison, and to her surprise, he'd opened up to her more than she'd expected he would, even about his thoughts on religion and the church when she'd asked. He was a nice young man, and it seemed he loved Zoe a lot, but it grieved her a little, no, a lot, that he didn't share her faith. She couldn't see a happy marriage ahead for them unless that changed. She sensed that Zoe had reconnected with God that morning in church, and that had made her heart glad. So many years of praying for her and holding her up to the Lord had finally paid off. Now she had another to be praying for. Harrison wasn't going to be easily swayed. He knew his mind and didn't see the need for God, but he had a need. Everyone did, whether they knew it or not, but it was up to God to work in his heart. All she could do was pray.

"Relieved?" Ruth raised a brow as she folded her arms and looked at the handsome young man sitting opposite her. She could see why Zoe loved him, but what was inside was more important.

He looked up, startled. "You heard?"

"I guessed." Ruth chuckled.

Harrison shook his head and chuckled with her.

"Yes. Very relieved."

"I told you there was nothing to worry about."

"You did, and seems you were right. Now, another drink?"

"Another cup of tea would be nice, thank you."

Chapter Nine

Zoe was asleep in a chair in the visitor lounge area when a shake of her shoulder stirred her. She opened her eyes slowly before sitting with a start.

"Mum! Harrison!" She looked at her watch and yawned. Just after midnight. "Did you just get here?"

Harrison nodded. "Fixing the car took longer than expected." He bent down and kissed her. "How are you doing, Zoe? You don't look too comfortable."

Zoe stretched, letting her hand rest on his arm. "No, it's not the best."

"How's Grandma?" Mum sat beside her and gave her a hug. Mum's eyes looked heavy and weary.

Zoe straightened and returned the hug. "She's resting, Mum. So far so good."

"Guess we can't see her until morning?"

Zoe shook her head. "No…"

"Let's get you home to bed, miss." Harrison extended his hand to Zoe and pulled her up, drawing her into an embrace.

"I'll stay here, just in case something happens," Mum said quietly.

Zoe looked down at her. How could she leave Mum here on her own? "I'll stay with you, Mum."

"You don't have to do that, Zoe. Go home and get

some rest. I'll be all right, and I'll call if anything changes."

"I can't do that, Mum. Let me stay." Zoe sat back down and took Mum's hand.

"You've been here for hours, Zoe. Go home and come back in the morning."

Zoe took a deep breath. It didn't sit right with her, leaving Mum on her own...

"I'll be fine, Zoe. Off you go. I'll call if anything changes."

She let out her breath. "Are you sure?"

"Absolutely."

"All right, then, but I'm not too happy about it. We'll be back first thing in the morning." Leaning forward, Zoe gave Mum another big hug.

"Sleep well, sweetheart." Mum pulled her tight. "Thanks for all you've done."

"It was nothing. I just pray Grandma pulls through."

"We all do, Zoe." Mum kissed Zoe's cheek and brushed some hair off her forehead before releasing her.

"Bye, Mum. See you in the morning." Zoe swallowed the lump in her throat as she smiled into Mum's glistening eyes.

Zoe leaned close to Harrison as they walked along the empty corridor towards the car park. "So what did you and Mum talk about for all that time?"

"Our secret." He looked down and kissed the top of her head.

She raised her head and smiled at him. It felt good to be in his arms, but that heavy weight in her stomach was still there. She tried to ignore it.

As they pulled up outside Zoe's apartment, Harrison slipped his arm around her shoulder and pulled her close. "Wish you'd let me stay, Zoe." He tipped her chin and gazed into her eyes.

She chuckled. "Tempting, but no." She leaned up and brushed his cheek with her hand. "It's important to me, Harrison, you know that."

He let out a resigned sigh. "I do, unfortunately." He placed his hand over hers, caressing her with his eyes. "I'm sorry, Zoe. I promise I won't pressure you anymore."

His tender words and tone sent warmth gushing through her body. She smiled at him. "Thank you." Leaning forward, she kissed him slowly, savouring the sweetness of his lips and the brush of his stubble against her cheek.

Pulling back, she smiled into his eyes. "See you in the morning—early." She slipped out of his arms and onto the pavement.

As the tail lights of Harrison's car disappeared around the corner, Zoe pressed her hands to her chest and prayed once more for him.

Zoe woke the next morning to loud knocking on the door. Lifting her head, she glanced at the clock and immediately her head fell back onto the pillow. She let out a frustrated sigh—how had she overslept?

Sliding out of bed, she threw on her robe before heading to the front door. Harrison stood there looking way too fresh, and with a playful grin on his face that made her want to throw her arms around his neck and kiss him. His left hand was behind his back.

"What have you got there?" Zoe angled her head and tried to see.

He whipped his hand around and presented her with a single soft pink rose. "A beautiful flower for my beautiful girl."

"Harrison, you're way too smooth! Which garden did you get that from?"

"Never you mind." He stepped closer and drew her into

his arms, brushing her messed up hair off her forehead. "Did you get enough sleep?"

Zoe stifled a yawn. "Not really, but I'll be okay."

He lowered his face and placed a gentle kiss on her lips. "Have you heard from your mum?"

She shook her head. "No, but we need to get going. Come in while I get ready."

Harrison stepped inside the small living room and headed straight for the kitchen. "Coffee?"

"Love one. I'll just take a quick shower."

Zoe quickly showered and dressed and returned to the kitchen just as Harrison was carrying two mugs of steaming coffee to the table.

"Should you call your mum?"

Sliding a bobby pin into her hair, she nodded. "Good idea, I'll grab my phone." Racing into her bedroom, she picked her iPhone up from the bedside table. Two missed calls from Mum and one message. Her heart plummeted. *How did I miss them?* She opened the message. *"Gran had a bad night. In surgery now. Please pray."* Zoe's stomach knotted and her mouth went dry. They couldn't lose Grandma now.

She sat on the edge of the bed and prayed. Her heart was heavy. *God, please help Grandma pull through. Be with her, and give the surgeon wisdom. And Lord, please still my heart and let me trust You like I know I should.*

"Zoe, what's wrong?" Harrison stood in the doorway, his head angled. "Is everything all right?"

Zoe shook her head, pushing back tears. "Grandma's in surgery now. She had a bad night." She could barely speak.

"Grab your purse, we'll go now." Harrison stepped forward, and extending his hand, helped her up.

Zoe gave him a grateful smile as she wiped her face. "Thanks."

She poured their coffees into travel mugs then ran out

the door after him.

The whole way to the hospital, Zoe's heart raced. She should be trusting God, but it seemed her faith wasn't as strong as it should be. The thought of losing Grandma tore at her heart—she wasn't ready for Grandma to go. Still so many things to ask her, to talk about… like what she should do about Harrison. Surely she'd get the chance. Zoe sniffed as she gazed out the window. She should have spent more time with her while she had the chance.

Even at this early hour, the hospital car park was almost full. Once they'd parked, Zoe slipped her hand into Harrison's as they half walked, half ran towards the ICU. Mum was seated by herself, and glanced up as they raced in. Her face was drawn. Zoe wasn't sure whether from lack of sleep or worry, or both.

Sitting beside her, Zoe gave Mum a big hug before searching her eyes. "How's Grandma?"

"Still waiting to hear. She's been in surgery just over two hours now."

"It could be a long operation."

"That's what they said."

"You should get some sleep, Mum."

"How can I sleep, Zoe? I need to be here."

Zoe squeezed Mum's hand. "I understand, but if you'd like a break, we'll call you if anything changes."

"Thanks, but I'll stay for now."

"Okay. At least let us get you some breakfast."

Mum lifted her eyes and smiled. "That would be nice."

"I'll get it." Harrison stood. "Stay here with your mum, Zoe."

Zoe smiled up at him gratefully and reached for his hand. "That's kind of you, Harrison. Thanks."

As Zoe watched him walk away, her heart warmed with love. He really was so thoughtful and kind.

"He's a nice man, Zoe." Mum reached out and squeezed her hand.

"I know."

"I'm praying for him."

Tears pricked Zoe's eyes. "Thanks."

They sat in silence with their hands joined until Harrison returned several minutes later carrying a tray stacked with food and polystyrene cups in each hand. Zoe greeted him with a warm smile. "Smells great!"

Raising his brows, Harrison chuckled. "Since when has hospital cafeteria food smelled great, Zoe?"

"Since when you're starving, that's when!"

He sat beside her. "Well, I hope this will be okay."

Mum gave him a sweet smile as she took a toasted sandwich and a coffee off the tray. "I'm sure it'll be fine. Thanks, Harrison."

Zoe was about to take a bite of her sandwich when a middle-aged male doctor approached and stood before them. The expression on his face said it all. Zoe dropped her sandwich and grabbed Mum's hand. This couldn't be happening. They couldn't have lost Grandma. She felt numb all over.

"Mrs. Taylor?" he asked of Mum.

Mum nodded.

"Would you like to come with me?" He turned, his gaze shifting between Zoe and Harrison. "Family?"

Zoe nodded. She couldn't speak.

"You're welcome to come, too."

Standing, Zoe placed her arm around Mum's shoulder, and together they walked along the corridor until they reached the small meeting room the doctor directed them to. Harrison followed along behind.

The room was sterile. Cold. The chairs scraped on the tiled floor as they were pulled out from the round, white table.

A picture featuring a bunch of yellow daisies sat on one wall, but wasn't enough to provide any level of cheer.

Zoe heard bits of the doctor's words. She herself might have to do this one day soon. Would she convey such bad news any differently? "We did our best...your mother's heart was in worse condition than we first thought...I'm sorry, but she didn't make it...she died on the table...I'm sorry for your loss." So routine, so devoid of emotion. How many times had he repeated those same words? It wasn't his fault. If anyone was to blame, it was their fault. They should have made Grandma take better care of herself. Made her see the doctor more often. Take it easier...

"What happens now? Can we see her?" Mum asked in a quiet voice.

"Of course, and then a nurse will go through the procedures with you. We did our best, Mrs. Taylor. I really am very sorry."

Holding a balled tissue to her nose, Mum nodded.

As Zoe leaned closer and placed her arm around Mum's shoulder, she was unable to contain her grief and wept openly.

Grandma looked peaceful. The pain that had been so heavily etched on her face during the trip to the hospital had gone. Zoe sat on a chair beside the bed and took Grandma's still warm hand in hers. Despite knowing that Grandma's soul had already left her and was now with Jesus, it was difficult not to talk to her as if she were still lying there in the bed.

Zoe's chest tightened as her eyes brimmed once more with tears. So many things she'd wanted to talk to Grandma about, but now it was too late. She squeezed Grandma's hand and gazed at her sweet face framed by her wispy silvery-grey hair. "I should have spent more time with you." Zoe sniffed. "I'm sorry, Grandma." Zoe wiped her eyes with the back of her hand. "You were a wonderful grandmother, and a wonderful person, and I love you." Leaning forward, Zoe placed a gentle kiss on Grandma's forehead. She sniffed. "Go in peace."

Zoe straightened slowly as a light hand settled on her shoulder. Without looking, she raised her hand and placed it on Harrison's, interweaving her fingers with his. Inhaling deeply, she took one last look at Grandma before she stood.

Harrison drew her into his arms and hugged her.

Clinging to him, Zoe sobbed into his shoulder.

He rubbed her back and wiped her tears with his fingers. "It's okay, Zoe. I'm here for you." His voice, soft and caring, gave her comfort and solace.

Zoe nodded as she drew another deep breath, turning her head and looking once more at Grandma before she left the room with Harrison's steadying arms around both her and Mum.

Chapter Ten

The next few hours passed in a blur. It hardly seemed real. Grandma was dead. After all the formalities at the hospital had been dealt with, Harrison drove Zoe and Mum back to Zoe's apartment. At the door, he took Zoe in his arms and brushed her hair back with his hand as he gazed into her eyes. "I'll be back soon, Zo. I need to visit my mum and my sisters."

"Say hello to them for me?"

"I will." He ran his fingers down her cheek. "Are you okay?"

Nodding, Zoe sucked in a breath. "I will be."

"Take it easy." He looked deep into her eyes.

She gave him a weary smile. "I'll try."

He kissed her gently before turning and jogging down the stairs.

Leaning against the door frame with her gaze fixed on Harrison's back, a wave of sadness enveloped Zoe. Grandma hadn't lived long enough to see her married. Zoe gulped. Would Grandma be happy with her choice? What would she advise her to do? Zoe lifted her hand in a wave as Harrison drove off and then pressed her hands to her chest. What did the future hold for them? Would Harrison respond to God? Or would she have to make a decision she knew she couldn't make? *God, I have to trust You with this…*

"You must be tired, Mum." Zoe said as she placed her

purse on the kitchen counter and switched on the kettle.

Mum let out a weary sigh and pulled out a chair. "Yes, but I doubt I could sleep."

"Maybe you should try. We can sort things later."

"But there's so much to organise, Zoe."

Zoe leaned back against the counter, tightening her pony tail before folding her arms. "I can make a start."

"I know what you're like, Zoe. You'll do everything if I let you."

"No I won't." Zoe lifted her chin. "I'll just make a list."

Mum sighed and looked at her with tired eyes, a half-smile lifting the corners of her mouth. "Promise?"

Zoe placed her hand over her heart. "I promise. Now, go and take a shower and have a sleep. I'll grab a clean towel and tidy the room."

"You don't need to tidy the room, Zoe."

Mum was right. The room was already tidy. "Okay. I'll just grab a towel."

"Thank you. And make sure you only make a list—nothing more, okay? I'll help when I get up."

"Okay." Zoe gave a reassuring smile before walking to the linen cupboard and pulling out a clean, white towel and matching flannel and handing them to Mum.

Mum lifted the towel to her face and rubbed it gently against her cheek. "Thank you, Zoe." Her eyes moistened.

"Oh, Mum." Zoe drew her close and hugged her.

"I'm sorry, Zoe. These remind me so much of Grandma. You use the same laundry liquid."

Zoe chuckled. "I always knew we were soul mates."

Mum wiped her tears. "I'm going to miss her."

"We all will."

"At least we know where she is."

Nodding, Zoe swallowed the lump in her throat. "Yes, we do." She released her hold on Mum. "Now, go and have that shower."

Mum stood and headed to the bathroom.

While Mum was in the shower, Zoe unpacked her bag that Harrison had quickly packed for her before he left the farm and put a load of washing on. Emma, her flat-mate, hadn't returned from her Christmas vacation yet, so the apartment was exactly how she'd left it. Neat and tidy, just the way she liked it.

Zoe looked up when Mum poked her head around the corner.

"I'll just have a short nap, Zoe."

"That's fine, Mum, take as long as you want."

Zoe made herself a cup of coffee, placing it on the side table before she flopped onto the couch. Sitting cross-legged, she grabbed a cushion and placed it on her lap, and then reached for her iPad and turned it on. She took a deep breath. Where to begin? The nurse at the hospital had been helpful, but there was still a lot to do, especially as Grandma's body needed to be transported back to Bellhaven so they could bury her beside Grandfather. Now it seemed like flying her to Brisbane might not have been such a good idea after all.

Leaning back against three neatly arranged matching cushions, Zoe drew a slow breath. They'd all been praying that Grandma would survive, but now she was dead. All their prayers had been in vain. Zoe's shoulders slumped. Why hadn't God heard them? Or had they been praying the wrong thing? The words from the sermon floated back to her... *"Your will, Your way, Your time"*. Was this God's will and God's time? Zoe let out a sigh. *Why couldn't You have let her live a little longer, God?* She gulped as she pushed back tears. *I'm sorry. That's me being selfish. I know she's in a better place, and that she's with You, but I can't help feeling sad that she's gone. I miss her already...*

Curling up on the couch, Zoe hugged a cushion to her chest and wept.

Harrison dialled his mum's phone number as he pulled out onto the road after leaving Zoe's place to let her know he was on his way. As soon as he pulled up outside the house he'd grown up in, Margaret ran out the door and hugged him. "Harrison, I'm so sorry this happened. Zoe must be so upset."

Harrison returned his mother's hug. "She's devastated. She really loved her Grandma."

"And you've had such a long drive. Come inside out of the heat. The girls are getting lunch ready." Margaret put her arm around Harrison's shoulder and bustled him inside.

He smiled warmly at her. "Thanks, Mum." He walked ahead of her to the kitchen, where his twin sisters, Chloe and Sophie, were busily preparing several salads for lunch. He gave them both a hug and accepted their condolences.

"The boys should be back any time now. They went out with Dad for that game of golf," Chloe said as she washed some tomatoes. "I told them they were crazy to be playing golf in this heat, but they didn't listen. I'm half expecting one of them to drop dead from heat exhaustion." She sucked in a breath as she covered her mouth with the tips of her fingers. "That was thoughtless of me. I'm sorry, Harrison."

"It's okay, Chloe."

"No, it's not. I'm always saying things I shouldn't." She put the tomatoes on the chopping board. "How's Zoe?"

"Upset, naturally, especially after flying with her Grandma all the way to Brisbane."

"Wow, she must know people in high places," Sophie said, bending down to pick up Lara-Katie, her seven month-old baby daughter who was trying to pull herself up on Sophie's leg.

What could he say to that? Yes, her ex-boyfriend just

happened to be in town with a plane, and he just happened to be a pilot with the Royal Flying Doctor Service? Would that sound petty? Probably. Best to keep it simple. "One of their neighbours had a plane."

"And you drove back with Zoe's mum?"

"Yep. The whole way."

Sophie chuckled. "That would have been fun."

"You could call it that. The car broke down."

Chloe laughed. "I don't believe it! She might not want you as a son-in-law now."

Harrison gulped. Maybe she didn't. Especially after he'd told her that he didn't think God was relevant for today's society. How had he been so stupid? He should have just pretended he was a believer. Kept her happy instead of giving her a reason to think he wasn't a suitable match for her daughter. Although she'd never said that. She just said she'd pray for him. He shook his head. Now it wasn't just his own mother praying for him, it was Zoe's mother too. *As well as Zoe.* Why did they all think he needed God, anyway? What was wrong with his life? How many times had he apologised to his mum for not speaking to her for all those years? Wasn't that enough?

"Harrison, is something wrong?" Chloe stepped closer, and putting her hands on his shoulders, peered into his eyes.

Harrison blinked. "No, no, sorry, something just crossed my mind, that's all. Everything's good."

"You sure? I know that look…"

"Yep, it's all good. Now, what can I do to help?"

"Set the table."

"I can do that."

As Harrison set the table for seven adults, he couldn't help but think about Zoe. Just three days ago he'd proposed to her in this very room, but it seemed like a lifetime had passed. So much had happened since then. The days following their engagement should have been filled with fun and lots of time together, not racing out to the farm because her parents had changed their plans. He wasn't annoyed by it, well, not much, just disappointed and a little frustrated. And now, with the funeral to plan and another trip to the farm, and then Zoe would be starting her Internship… He let out a sigh. *Guess I've just got to go along with it all.*

Male voices entering the front door pulled him from his thoughts. He placed the last knife on the table and sauntered down the hallway to meet them with his hands in his pockets.

"Harrison, we missed you!" Alastair clapped Harrison's back with his hot hand.

"Glad I didn't go, looking at all of you! Your shirts won't need washing, they're soaked already." Harrison laughed.

"And I can smell them from here," Sophie called out from the kitchen.

Harrison had to agree. The body odour rising from the three hot, sweaty men was enough to make even his eyes water, and that was saying something. As a veterinary surgeon, he was used to foul smells, but this was worse.

"We get the message, we're not wanted," Harold, Harrison's father, said as he closed the door.

Poking her head around the corner, Sophie held her nose and made a face. "I didn't mean it like that, Dad. But yes, you do stink."

"We'd better take a shower, then," Harold said.

"Good idea." Margaret stood at the end of the hallway with her arms crossed. "You're not coming any further until you do."

"Bossy!" Laughing, Alastair headed towards the bathroom.

Even though they lived in England, Alastair and Angus both had a great relationship with his parents. Harrison wondered whether his relationship with Zoe's parents would be like this, or would a wedge come between them if he didn't follow their faith? He suspected the latter, although right now they seemed friendly enough. Why couldn't it be simple? He just wanted to marry Zoe, that was all.

"Harrison, come and give a hand," Chloe called from the kitchen.

His eyes widened as she took a three layered sponge cake decorated with cream and strawberries from the fridge and placed it on the counter.

"It's for Alastair's and Angus's birthday. I just need to finish decorating it before lunch."

"What do you want me to do?"

"Keep them out of here."

"No problem." That was easy—he'd put the cricket on. Australia was playing Pakistan at the Melbourne Cricket Ground. He flicked on the television and sat back on a recliner and put his feet up. All he needed now was a beer, but no use asking—Mum wouldn't give him one at this time of day. She was very set in her ways. She didn't mind him drinking, but only at dinner. At least Zoe didn't mind him having the occasional beer in the afternoon.

"What's the score?" Alastair was out first. He stood in the doorway with one towel hugging his hips and another in his hands drying his hair.

"Australia's got three more wickets to get."

"They'll do that, easy."

"Not so sure. Kahloon and Singh are batting—don't like their chances." Harrison sat forward and let out a roar. "Singh's gone for twenty."

"What'd I tell you?" Alastair stepped into the room and perched on the edge of the couch.

"They were lucky."

"No, Harris is a great bowler. The English team's wary of him."

"Yeah, he's pretty good."

"Alastair! What are you doing sitting on the couch in your towel? Mum will have a fit!"

Alastair jumped up. "Sorry, Chlo—forgot where I was."

She glared at him. "You'd better get dressed. Lunch is just about ready."

"Onto it." He popped a kiss on her lips as he slipped past her.

Harrison chuckled at the banter between the two, and all of a sudden he just wanted Zoe to be here.

Lunch passed with general chit-chat and questions directed at Harrison about the trip to and from the farm, and plans for Zoe's Grandma's funeral.

He shrugged. "Don't know much yet, apart from the funeral being out in the country."

"A pity she was flown to Brisbane in the first place," Sophie said as she picked up her glass of sparkling mineral water.

Exactly what he was thinking. Maybe having Spencer around had caused Zoe to act rashly. Would anyone else have considered asking someone to fly them to hospital? He doubted it. Not even Ruth or Kevin. They would have waited for the doctor. "Guess you never know in situations like these. Zoe did what she thought best at the time."

"You're right. She obviously didn't want her Gran to die," Chloe said.

"No, not at all. She's devastated." Harrison put down his fork, and leaning forward, rested his elbows on the table and steepled his fingers. "I remember when Granddad died, we were all upset for ages. I was only ten, but I remember it clearly. A pity I didn't get to know him better."

"He was a good man, your Granddad," Harold said. "Didn't like me to start with, stealing his daughter away from him," Harold's eyes twinkled as he glanced at Margaret, "but I soon got him on my side."

"How d'you do that, Dad?" Chloe asked, angling her head.

"Ah," he chuckled, "I made sure she got home early every night, and I always called him 'sir'." He chuckled again. "He liked that."

Harrison sighed. That wouldn't work for him. He'd have to think of some other way of keeping Zoe's parents onside. *Apart from becoming religious.*

Chloe gathered the dirty plates and carried them into the kitchen. She returned a few minutes later with the cake, protecting the lit candles with her hand. Everyone cheered as twin brothers, Alastair and Angus, looked up with surprised expressions on their faces.

Two-year old Lachlan climbed up on his dad's lap. "Lachy blow candles?"

Everyone laughed as they began to sing "Happy Birthday".

"You can help Daddy blow them out." Together, Alastair, Lachlan and Angus blew the candles out in one go. Lachlan clapped his hands and everyone laughed again.

Harrison grew quiet as he studied father and son. Zoe had never mentioned if she wanted children or not. And he himself hadn't really thought about it until now, but seeing the way Alastair connected with Lachlan, and Angus with Lara-Katie, made him think it might be nice. But would Zoe give up her career as a doctor, after all the study she'd put in, to raise children? He gulped. After all, hadn't that been why he'd stopped talking with his parents when his mother was always away with her job as a journalist instead of being there for him and his sisters when they were growing up? He understood why she'd done it now… she wanted to give him and his sisters a better life than she'd had, but did he still hold the same belief that mothers shouldn't work? Maybe deep down, he did. Zoe would never agree with that. He had some soul searching to do.

Margaret leaned closer and placed her hand lightly on Harrison's arm. "We were thinking we'd go down to the bay late this afternoon and have dinner by the water. Do you think Zoe and her mum would like to join us?"

Harrison jolted himself out of his thoughts and smiled at her. "I think they'd like the fresh air. I'll give Zoe a call."

When Harrison phoned Zoe shortly after, she agreed on one condition…that they ride their bicycles there.

He let out an exasperated sigh. Riding to the bay was the last thing he felt like doing, especially after such a big lunch. "But Zoe, it's such a long way, and it's still so hot. Can't we drive?"

"It'll do us good, Harrison. I need to do something physical. Mum can drive my car so we can put the bikes on the back to come home."

He let out another sigh, but couldn't help himself from chuckling. "Okay, you win. I'll be there soon." Maybe a ride would do them good, release some tension, but to be honest, he would much rather drive. But he'd do it to keep her happy.

Chapter Eleven

By the time Harrison arrived back at Zoe's place, she was ready to leave. Dressed in her black and green lycra riding outfit, Harrison could hardly take his eyes off her shapely figure. She was tying back her long auburn hair, and he walked over and gave her a kiss on the cheek. "Missed you." If Ruth wasn't sitting on the couch he would have pulled her close and kissed her long and hard, but after what he'd heard at his parents' table, keeping his hands off her was one way of staying in Ruth's good graces.

"And I missed you too." She raised one brow as her gaze drifted from his head down to his feet. "See you're dressed for the occasion."

Harrison glanced down at his shorts. "What's wrong with what I'm wearing?"

"Thought you might have worn the gear I bought you for your birthday."

She had a point. He hadn't had the nerve to tell her he wouldn't be seen dead in lycra. But he had an excuse. "I didn't have time to go home." He smiled apologetically. "Next time."

"Okay, guess it'll have to do." She finished tying her hair and then sat on the couch, stretching first her left leg, and then her right. "Sure you'll be all right, Mum?"

"Yes, Zoe, I'll be fine. I'll follow the directions you put into my phone."

Harrison chuckled. Zoe couldn't help herself if she tried.

"We'll go then, and we'll see you there." She bent down and kissed her mum.

Ruth looked a little fresher than earlier, but her eyes were still rimmed in red. She gave Zoe a warm smile and squeezed her hand. "Ride safely, Zoe."

"We will, Mum. Don't worry about us."

"Bye, Ruth, see you there." Harrison lifted his hand in a wave before placing his hand on the small of Zoe's back.

"Bye, Harrison, take care."

Harrison followed Zoe down the back steps to where she'd left the bikes. Hers was an expensive road bike, light and well appointed. With twenty-one gears, she could fly up just about any hill without slowing down. His was much heavier and nowhere near as fast. To keep up with her he had to work really hard. Just what he needed on a hot day like today. Maybe he should spend some money and get a better one, but that wouldn't help right now.

As Zoe clipped on her helmet, he stepped closer and caught her in his arms. He unclipped her helmet, and lowering his head, pressed his lips hard against hers.

"Harrison!" She sounded breathless as she tried to push him away.

He looked deeply into her eyes. "I missed you, Zoe."

She laughed. "It's only been a few hours."

"I know. But it wasn't the same without you there."

"You're just a big softy, Harrison. Let's go."

"I'm not." He lifted his chin.

"Yes, you are." She laughed as she re-clipped her helmet.

He sighed as he placed his on his head. "Are you sure we can't go in the car?

The amused glint in her eye provided the answer.

He chuckled as he threw his leg over the saddle and placed his foot on the pedal. "Okay, let's go. You lead—I don't want to slow you down."

"Don't be petty."

"I'm not being petty."

"Yes, you are." She looked back at him as she took off.

Harrison shook his head and laughed. He'd never win an argument with her.

Zoe slipped her shoe under the strap and kicked down a couple of gears as she quickly built up speed. The air was thick and hot on her face, but she almost didn't feel it. She glanced back at Harrison. He was just one bike length behind. So far, so good. Why didn't he get a new bike? That old clunker of his was barely fit for a slow Sunday ride along the river, let alone a long ride out to the bay. Oh well, his decision.

She put her hand out to turn right, checking both ways before she crossed. There was more traffic than she'd expected, but at least it was moving. Once in the separate bike lane, Zoe increased her speed further. Before long, some of the tension in her body slipped away. Harrison wouldn't keep up, but maybe a sprint would help clear the ache in her heart.

Adrenalin pumped through her body as the wind hit her face. She tried to swallow, but her throat was dry. Slowing a little, she reached for her water bottle and took a gulp. Glancing back, Harrison wasn't in sight. She let out a slow breath. She'd better wait. He wouldn't be impressed as it was. She slowed right down to a snail's pace. He should be catching her any time now. As the seconds ticked by, she began to worry. What if he'd come off? Or got a puncture? She glanced back again. Still not there. She let out a sigh. Better go back. Just as she was turning, he came into view. She shook her head as he approached. "We're not out for a Sunday picnic, you know!"

"It might not be a Sunday, but we are out for a picnic." He chuckled as he pedalled past her, maintaining a steady, but slow, pace. "Besides, what's the hurry?" He laughed as he built up speed and pulled ahead before she could turn around again to catch up.

She was breathless when she pulled alongside. "So I guess you think that was funny?"

He slowed down and shrugged. "Yeah, it felt good to be in front for once."

"You should get a new bike."

"I agree. Maybe I will." He flashed her a smile that warmed her heart.

The rest of the way they rode either alongside each other where the roads or path permitted, or in close single file with Harrison leading the way when it didn't. He raised his brows when she suggested he take the lead, but she felt good about it. For once, she could watch him instead of having his eyes on her all the time. Finally the air cooled a little, and when the first glimpse of the bay came into view, Zoe called out to Harrison to pull over. She got off her bike and removed her helmet, wiping her moist face with the back of her hand.

The bay glistened in the lazy afternoon sun, a deep shade of blue as it reflected the colour of the sky. In the distance, North Stradbroke Island stretched out for miles in either direction, and other smaller islands dotted the water in between. A number of sail boats had their spinnakers out as they headed back in after a day out on the water, and the car ferry from Straddie, laden with holiday-makers, chugged along on its way to the island.

"Maybe we could go to Straddie for our honeymoon?" Harrison slipped his arms around Zoe's waist from behind, working his lips gently down her neck, sending shivers through her body.

Zoe turned around and brought her arms up around his neck. Dropping her head back, his lips trailed upwards toward her face until she tipped her chin and his lips found hers.

Harrison's kiss left Zoe in no doubt of his love for her. She just had to trust God to work out the rest.

Leaning back in his arms, she glanced at the sky. Dark clouds had formed to the south. Was God about to answer their prayers for rain? And if He did, would it reach all the way out to Bellhaven?

Shortly after, they pulled into the park where they were meeting his family. Surprisingly, they were the first ones there, so they bought ice-creams and sat on a seat, holding hands and laughing at the antics of several small children trying to catch sea gulls. By the time everyone arrived, the weight in Zoe's heart had lightened, and she finally felt she could enjoy being engaged to the most intelligent, loving man she'd ever known without feeling guilty. Somehow God was going to work this out. She didn't know how, but somehow He would. She just had to trust Him.

The picnic by the bay was just what Zoe and her mum needed. The fresh sea air washed away some of their grief and helped prepare them for the long days ahead.

Chapter Twelve

Later that night, Zoe slipped her hands around Harrison's neck as he leaned back against his car. A cool evening breeze touched her cheek and neck and made her shiver, but she wasn't about to complain. It just meant Harrison pulled her closer, and that was fine by her.

"I have to go into work tomorrow, Zoe. It's Tessa's last day and she needs to do a hand-over." Harrison brushed her hair with his hand as he gazed into her eyes.

"Well, Mum and I are meeting with the Funeral Transfer company in the morning, and then we've got a telephone meeting with the Funeral director at Bellhaven after that. And I want to go to the bank with Mum." Zoe took a breath and raised her chin. "They're not going to get away with this, Harrison. I'm going to fight them to the end."

Harrison's eyes twinkled with amusement. "I love it when you get feisty, Zoe, but you can't fight everyone's battles."

"No, but I'll fight for justice for my parents. You'd do the same, wouldn't you?"

He smiled. "I guess so. Well, I hope it goes well. I'll be thinking of you."

She returned his smile. "Thanks."

He linked his hands around her waist. "How about just you and I go out for dinner tomorrow night before you head back to the farm?"

"That sounds wonderful, Harrison." Zoe's expression grew serious. "I'm sorry for being so short sometimes."

His face twisted into a playful grin. "You're not short, Zoe. You're almost as tall as me."

She chuckled as she tapped the back of his head with her hand. "Funny."

His expression grew serious. "Goodnight my sweet. See you tomorrow night." His brown eyes softened as he brought his hand to her face, pulling her closer until his lips brushed hers.

His kiss was so gentle, and as he pulled her closer, she felt his love flowing deep into her soul.

When he drove off soon after, Zoe pressed her hands to her chest and savoured the lingering taste of him on her lips. Her heart felt as light as the leaves wafting along the path in the gentle breeze. Thunder echoing in the distance aroused her senses further, and made her long for the day when Harrison could stay. Shaking her hair loose, she let it play on her shoulders and imagined Harrison was still holding her, caressing her, kissing her. The moment passed and she laughed at herself before turning and running lightly up the steps.

Mum was already in bed, so Zoe poured herself a glass of chilled mineral water and tip-toed out onto the balcony. Her legs were sore and tired after the bike ride, but her mind wouldn't stop. So many things to organise and sort, Grandma's funeral being one of them. And Mum had asked her to give the eulogy.

Zoe glanced up at the star speckled sky just in time to see a shooting star zooming across the darkness before it disappeared into oblivion. Words Grandma had spoken to her when she was younger drifted through her mind... *Take time to smell the roses, dear.* Zoe smiled as she gazed up into the clear night sky, the storm clouds having moved out to sea. *Yes, Grandma, I'll try. In fact, I'll go smell the rose Harrison gave me this morning.* And with that, she turned and went inside, picking up the now fully opened pink rose she'd placed in a tall, slender vase just this morning. Inhaling its sweet perfume, warm thoughts of both Harrison and Grandma flowed through her mind.

Zoe's alarm bleated at six a.m. Knowing she'd be tempted to hit snooze, she'd placed her phone on her bookshelf, just out of reach so she'd have to get up. Climbing out of bed, she stood and turned it off. She stretched her neck before peeking out the blind. Already the sun's rays were beating down on the city. Another hot day, but she needed to run. After the bike ride yesterday, she was determined to regain her fitness, and running every morning would be part of her new regime, as well as a long bike ride every other day. She changed into her lycra shorts and top, slipped on her Nikes, and opened her bedroom door.

Mum was already up and dressed, and sitting at the table reading her Bible. She looked up and smiled. "Good morning, Zoe. Going for a run?"

Zoe held her arms above her head and stretched to the left. "Thought I would, if you don't mind."

"Fine by me, love. I can look after myself."

"I won't be long." Zoe finished her stretch, and stepping closer, popped a kiss on Mum's cheek. As she did, her eyes caught a highlighted verse in Mum's Bible. *"And this same God who takes care of me will supply all your needs from His glorious riches, which have been given to us in Christ Jesus."* Zoe straightened, placing a hand on her hip. She pointed to the verse with the index finger of her other hand. "I'm struggling to understand how God can be looking after you when you're about to lose the farm."

"Maybe He doesn't want us to keep it, Zoe."

Zoe's eyes widened. "How can you even think that, Mum? Why would God want you turned out of your home?

"I don't know, but I do know He'll provide for us one way or the other."

"It sounds to me like you're giving up."

"No, we're not, but we have to consider our options."

Zoe angled her head. Options? How could her parents be considering *options?* "Like what?"

Mum shrugged. "I'm not sure yet."

"Well, I'm going to do my best to help you keep it. I'd like to pay the bank a visit today."

Mum smiled wistfully as she placed her hand on Zoe's wrist. "They won't budge, Zoe."

"It has to be worth a try." Zoe squared her shoulders. "Will you come with me?"

Mum sighed heavily. "It'll be a waste of time, Zoe, but okay. I can't let you go on your own."

Smiling, Zoe squeezed Mum's hand. "Guess we'll see if it's a waste of time. Anyway, I think I'll go for that run. Get geared up for the day. I won't be long."

Minutes later, Zoe's feet pounded the pavement as she jogged along the path winding down to the river. Other runners were out, and she nodded as they passed each other. She normally listened to her favourite radio station when she jogged, but today she needed a clear head. Especially when it came to the bank. How could Mum and Dad even be considering options? What were they thinking? Surely God wouldn't allow them to be turned out of their home. Zoe slowed to take a corner, but struggled to build up pace again. After yesterday's ride her legs still felt heavy, and the air was already thick with humidity and she was finding it hard to breathe. Stopping and bending forward, she pressed her hands to her thighs and gulped in mouthfuls of air.

A shadow loomed and stopped beside her. "Hot day," a familiar voice said.

Jerking up, Zoe sucked in a breath as she looked straight into Spencer's amused eyes. "Spencer, what are you doing here? Thought you'd be back home by now." She pressed her hand to her chest and tried to steady her breathing.

He ran his hand across his blond hair. "Decided to take a few days in the city. Catch up with some friends." He shrugged before his expression sobered. "How's your Grandma doing?"

Zoe's heart plummetted. How could she tell Spencer his mercy dash had been in vain? But she had to, no use lying. He'd find out anyway. She took a deep breath and gulped. "She didn't make it, Spencer." Zoe's voice came out little and weak and caught in her throat, and before she knew it, tears streamed down her cheeks.

He stepped closer and drew his arm around her. "I'm so sorry, Zoe. You did your best."

"But it wasn't enough." Zoe sobbed. Why was she letting it out now? She'd managed to hold her tears mainly at bay with Mum and Harrison. Maybe it was the memory of the adrenalin rush she and Spencer shared as they flew Grandma to hospital, and of the sheer desperation to get her there as quickly as possible, and the fact that it had been in vain, but whatever it was, she sobbed into his shoulder.

He stroked her hair. "She's with the Lord now, Zoe. Take comfort from that."

Nodding, Zoe sucked in a breath and pulled away. She swiped her wrist sweatband across her eyes and sniffed. "You're right, Spencer. I just wasn't ready to lose her just yet."

He squeezed her shoulder. "She was a wonderful woman, Zoe." He met her gaze and held it, compassion and empathy oozing from his eyes. "You're very much like her. Strong, resilient, hard-working, determined."

Zoe's body shuddered as another wave of sobs threatened to rack her body. How much longer could she stand here eye to eye with Spencer without doing something foolish? The physical attraction between them was like a magnet, and the memories they shared, too vivid. If only he hadn't broken the promise he'd made to her when she was sixteen. But he had, and now it was too late.

"I need to go, Spencer. We've got a funeral to organise."

"Can I help? I could arrange for a transfer if you need one. I guess that's the plan?"

Zoe's chin dropped. What would Harrison think if she accepted more help from Spencer? She sighed. No, best stick to the plan. "That's kind of you, Spencer, but Mum and I are meeting with the transfer company this morning, so I think it's all in hand."

"Okay, as long as you're sure. Let me know if you run into any trouble." He turned to go, but then stopped. "I almost forgot to tell you…I've been doing some research on that guy, and I'm getting close to finding him."

Despite herself, Zoe chuckled. "Already? Wow, you still act fast."

Spencer shrugged. "Some things don't change, Zoe."

"Seems they don't." She raised a brow, shaking her head and letting out another small chuckle. "You beat me to this one." She'd dropped her game, obviously. When they were teenagers, she and Spencer were always competing to see who was the smartest and the quickest at just about everything. Well, seems he'd won this one, but she didn't mind if it meant her parents might get their money back.

"I haven't got him yet."

"No, but you will. Let me know as soon as you find him." She pursed her lips. "I want to take him for all he's got."

"You've still got fire in your belly, Zoe. You're stirred up about this, aren't you?"

"You could say that. He's ruined my parents' lives."

Spencer's expression softened. "Sometimes you just have to accept what is, Zoe. You never know what God might have in store for them."

Zoe's eyes narrowed. Why was everyone giving up hope? She wouldn't give up until every last stone had been turned. "Easy for you to say, Spencer, it's not your parents being turned out of their home."

"I understand that, but take it easy, okay? Be prepared to listen to God, Zoe. And besides, you don't want to burn out, especially not this year."

He was right—this year was going to be a shocker. But still…

"I'll think about it, Spencer. Anyway, I must go." She stepped closer and touched his arm. As she did, a current ran up her arm and through her body. She sighed. She should have kept her distance.

"Might see you back home then. Take care, Zoe." His blue eyes smiled at her.

"You too, Spencer." Forcing a smile, she lifted her hand and waved as she began to jog slowly back the way she'd come.

Harrison's eyes sprung open as he turned onto the riverside esplanade. A young woman looking very much like Zoe was hugging a well-built blond-haired man who looked very much like Spencer. *No! it can't be…* He took another look and his heart plummetted. His eyes hadn't deceived him.

He thumped the wheel. *Why would Zoe be doing this?* His lips were still raw from last night's kisses. *How could she be in another man's arms this morning!* She'd convinced him nothing was going on between the two of them. He didn't understand. A mixture of despair, anger and confusion welled up within him.

How could he go to work now and talk calmly with Tessa as if nothing had happened? Maybe he should call off the meeting and reschedule, and instead confront Zoe and find out what was going on. He let out an angry sigh. No, Tessa had said it had to be today. He'd just have to confront Zoe tonight at dinner.

Harrison swung into the car park of the New Farm Veterinary Clinic a few minutes early. Tessa had asked him to be there by seven as she had a busy day finishing off everything before she and her husband, Ben, left for Ecuador the following morning. He closed the roof and stepped out of the car. A cigarette right now would help, but he didn't have any—Zoe had made him give up smoking soon after they'd started dating. Without one at hand, he paced the length of the car park. *What was Zoe playing at?* He raked his hand through his hair. He just couldn't understand her. Maybe it was all too hard and they should just call it off. But that thought made him sick in the stomach. Zoe was everything he'd ever wanted in a girl. Smart, funny, loyal, kind, beautiful. Maybe a little too feisty at times, and perhaps a little too bossy, but what they had was special. Well, he thought it was. He loved her, and he thought she loved him. If she was still hankering after Spencer, then she should come clean. Not kiss him passionately one night and fall into Spencer's arms the next. He hadn't thought she was that kind of girl.

Tessa's small blue sedan pulled into the car park and stopped beside his car. As she opened the car door and stepped out, she waved and walked towards him, a genuine smile lighting up her face. How she could be happy when things were such a mess for her and her husband? Maybe they'd heard from Ben's son?

"How are you, Harrison?"

Harrison squared his shoulders and forced himself to return her smile. "Fine, thanks. And you?"

"Busy, but good." She inserted the key into the door and pushed it open.

She turned on the air-con while he opened the blinds. The smell of disinfectant wafted in the air but didn't fully disguise the distinctive odour left behind by the dog and cat clientele.

"You must be excited," Harrison said as he turned around.

Tessa nodded. "And a little nervous."

"It'll be a great adventure."

"We hope so." She smiled at him again as she motioned for him to head into her office.

His eye was drawn to the photo of Tessa, her husband, Ben, their son, Jayden, and their two dogs, taken on one of the local beaches not long after Tessa and Ben's wedding. Who would have thought that everything could go so wrong for them?

"You look a little on edge, Harrison. Is everything all right?"

Harrison clenched his jaw. How could Tessa have already noticed? Was it that obvious? He shrugged. "Just a few issues, that's all."

Tessa angled her head, flicking her light brown hair over her shoulder. "With what? Surely not with Zoe? She was over the moon when you proposed."

That's what he'd thought, too, until God and Spencer came on the scene. He didn't have to tell Tessa everything. "Her Grandma died, and things have gotten a bit complicated, that's all."

Tessa's expression softened. "I'm sorry to hear that, Harrison. Such a sad thing to happen at Christmas."

"Yes. It's been hard on the whole family."

"I bet. Is Zoe okay?"

Harrison rubbed his neck. "She will be."

Tessa met his gaze and held it. "Is everything okay between the two of you? I'm sensing there's more than you're telling me."

Harrison shook his head and exhaled. "How do you do that Tessa? You seem to have this sixth sense about you."

She let out a small chuckle. "I'm not quite sure about that, but your downcast face offered a good clue. I would have thought you'd be on cloud nine having just gotten engaged."

He glanced out the window and then leaned his elbows on the desk, lifting his gaze to meet hers. "You win. There is something else." He drew a long breath and gulped. "I saw Zoe hugging an old flame this morning."

Tessa laughed. "Why do you men always jump to the worst possible scenario without bothering to find out the truth?" She leaned forward and lightly touched his wrist, holding her gaze steady. "Zoe loves you, Harrison. I've seen it in the way she looks at you. She'd never cheat on you—she's not that kind of girl."

"I didn't think so, either, but you didn't see her. They looked pretty close to me."

"Talk to her about it, Harrison. Don't let anything like this come between you. Misunderstandings can grow out of all proportion if you don't nip them in the bud early. Believe me, I know."

"I'll give it some thought." He leaned back and folded his arms. "She won't set a date either." He didn't need to tell her why.

Rolling her eyes, Tessa let out a chuckle and then folded her arms on the desk as she leaned closer to him. "What do you expect? You've only just gotten engaged. Plus her Grandma's just died, and she's got a huge year ahead." Her voice grew serious. "Don't push her, Harrison. Just let her enjoy being in love without adding to the pressure."

He shook his head. It wasn't true. He hadn't been pressuring her…or had he?

Tessa straightened and put on her business-like face. "Now we've got that sorted, we need to do this hand-over. It shouldn't take long."

For the next hour or so, Harrison took notes and absorbed all the information Tessa gave him. Being manager didn't phase him as much as it did Tessa. Maybe he could talk Fran, the owner, into letting them swap jobs. How many times had Tessa tried to muscle in on his surgery? He sensed she'd be happier in her old job as Head Surgeon than Clinic Manager.

When they finished, Tessa stood and tidied her desk.

An awkward moment passed between them. Should he hug her, or just shake hands? Their relationship had changed since Tessa had intervened a while back and had been the catalyst for fixing the rift between him and his mum. Plus she'd been there when he proposed to Zoe. He stepped forward and held out his hand, but as he did, Tessa looked up and instead of taking his hand, hugged him.

"You'll do a good job, Harrison, I know you will. And take care of Zoe."

"Thanks Tessa. I hope all goes well for you and Ben."

"We hope so, too." She released her hold, brushing back a tear that had slipped from her eye. She let out a small chuckle. "I just had a thought go through my mind. What if Zoe had seen you just then? What would she think?" She raised her brow. "See how easily things can be misconstrued?"

"Maybe you're right." But he wasn't convinced. It hadn't looked innocent to him.

Tessa smiled. "Okay, we're all done. See you in a few months!"

"Good luck, Tessa." He raised his hand in a wave as he exited her office. He smiled to himself. *His office.*

Chapter Thirteen

"How can you do that, Mr. Roberts? My parents have been customers of this bank for almost forty years, and you're going to take not only their home, but their livelihood from them, just like that! I don't know how you can sleep at night!"

Mum placed a hand lightly on Zoe's wrist.

Zoe shrugged it off. She wasn't going to let the bank win that easily. "Okay, withdraw five thousand dollars from my account and transfer it into their account. My fiancé will put in another five."

The bank manager's round eyes widened. "Unless you've got a lot more money to follow, Miss Taylor, it'll be a waste of your money."

"Let me decide that."

He raised a brow as he tapped his keyboard. "Five thousand?"

Stifling a gulp, Zoe nodded. She'd intended to transfer the full ten thousand, but the funeral costs were higher than expected, and Mum had nothing to put towards it.

"Done." Mr. Roberts looked first at Zoe and then at Mum. "That gives you a few extra weeks, Mrs. Taylor. I hope you can find the money somewhere, but there's nothing more we can do. We can't allow you to get further into debt."

Narrowing her eyes, Zoe leaned forward "Talking of that, why did you lend my parents money for an investment that didn't exist?"

Mr. Roberts folded his arms and adopted a superior manner. "It was a lo-doc loan, Miss. Taylor. Your parents took the risk upon themselves."

Zoe opened her mouth then closed it. She turned to face Mum, her brows puckering. Surely they hadn't done that? Why didn't they tell her?

Mum lowered her head and fiddled with the tissue in her hands.

"Is that true, Mum? Did you do it without getting the bank to check it?"

Mum raised her head and nodded. "We thought it was too good an opportunity to pass up." Her eyes watered. "We were wrong."

Mr. Roberts cleared his throat. "Any chance of getting the money back, Mrs. Taylor?"

Zoe butted in. "I've got a friend looking for the guy."

"Good luck with that. Those types seem to disappear into thin air."

"If you'd done your job properly, Mr. Roberts, they wouldn't have lost their money in the first place."

Mr. Roberts fixed his gaze firmly on her. "Watch what you're saying, Miss Taylor. You could find yourself in court."

Zoe's nostrils flared. "And so might you!" As she stood, the chair tipped backwards, making a loud noise as it landed on the tiled floor. "Come on, Mum, let's get out of here."

Outside, Zoe sucked in several deep breaths. "That man! The hide of him!"

"Calm down, Zoe. It was our fault. We should have been more careful."

"Don't say that, Mum. They were wrong to lend you money when they knew what your situation was."

Tears welled in Mum's eyes again. "It wasn't as bad back then." She pulled a fresh tissue from her purse and dabbed her eyes. "But Zoe, it's okay. God will look after us. I wish you hadn't put your money in. You should have used it for your wedding."

"It's okay. We can earn more." She cupped Mum's elbow and directed her down the street. "Come on, let's get a coffee. I need one after being with that man."

"He was just doing his job."

"Stop being so accommodating, Mum. Stand up for yourself."

"We're tired, Zoe."

Letting out a frustrated sigh, Zoe glanced at her mother. She did look tired, but Grandma dying would have contributed to that. "You can't just give in."

"God has a plan."

Zoe let out another sigh. She'd have to discuss that with God later.

Early that evening, Zoe slipped on her favourite summer dress and dabbed some of the Eternity perfume Harrison had given her for Christmas on her wrists and behind her ears. Leaning closer to the mirror, she applied a light coat of mascara and touched up her lipstick. Pointless putting much else on in this heat—it'd slide off within a few minutes, but she did want to look nice for her date with Harrison. It seemed so long since they'd spent time on their own, and now she was heading back to the farm in the morning with Mum, it might be days, possibly longer, before they'd see each other again.

"You look lovely, dear," Mum said when Zoe stepped out of the bathroom and into the living room. "I love that colour on you."

"Thanks, Mum." Zoe ran her hands down her emerald-green figure hugging dress and couldn't agree more. Taking her leather purse off the counter, she slipped it over her shoulder. "Are you sure you'll be okay on your own?"

"Yes, dear, I'll be fine. I'll do some reading and give Dad a call."

"Give him my love."

"I will. Enjoy your night." Mum gave Zoe a warm smile. "And Zoe…"

Zoe paused, tilting her head.

"Thanks for trying today with the bank. I probably didn't sound grateful enough—I'm sorry."

"Oh, Mum, it's okay. I can't imagine what you're going through."

"It's Dad and Peter I'm worried about, but I'm sure God will look after us."

There it was again. Maybe God should send rain or help them get their money back, but right now, it seemed it was up to her to save the farm.

Zoe gave a half-smile as she leaned down and placed a kiss on Mum's cheek. "I'm sure He will."

A soft knock sounded on the door. Zoe checked her watch. *Right on time.* "Don't wait up, Mum."

"Okay. Have a nice time, dear."

"Thanks."

Opening the door, Zoe smiled expectantly, but as her eyes met Harrison's, her smile slipped. He kissed her cheek, but his eyes were heavy and dark and his smile seemed forced. Maybe he'd just had a bad day at work.

Stepping closer, she lifted her hand to his cheek and ran it lightly down his stubble. "What's up, Harrison?"

His eyes remained focused and steady. "Not here, Zoe."

"Right." She closed the door behind her. "Where are we going?"

"I booked a table at a new restaurant at Southbank." His voice was clipped.

"That sounds nice." Zoe forced herself to stay upbeat, although her heart raced.

He opened the car door for her and she slid under his arm. His whole body seemed tense, and she just wanted to find out what was wrong, but she didn't want to force it either.

She did her seatbelt up and looked at him. "How was your day?"

"It was okay. How did yours go?" He started the engine and accelerated faster than normal down the road.

"The funeral's sorted. Mum and I leave in the morning. But no joy with the bank."

He glanced at her. "Did you really expect any?"

"I thought they might have given a bit, so yes."

"Well, I'm not surprised." He slowed down for a red light and tapped the steering wheel with his fingers.

"What's wrong, Harrison? Something's eating you." She hadn't meant to ask again, but not knowing was driving her crazy.

"I saw you this morning."

Zoe drew her eyebrows together. "This morning? Where?" She'd been lots of places, and why was seeing her a problem, anyway? And then the penny dropped. *He'd seen her with Spencer.* She felt ill.

"On the esplanade. Hugging Spencer."

"It's not what it looked like, Harrison."

He accelerated as the lights changed to green and looked at her with one eye. "What was it like, then?"

How could she explain? Her heart thumped. Harrison would never believe it was an accidental meeting, but she had to try. "We just bumped into each other."

He turned his head. His brow was raised and lips flat. "Right. And you just happened to bump into his arms?"

Zoe gulped. "I was upset about Grandma. He was just comforting me."

Silence. "I don't like it, Zoe. It seems too much of a coincidence."

"Nothing's going on between us, Harrison. If you don't believe me, maybe we shouldn't be engaged." As soon as she said it, she wished she could take back the words. But she wasn't going to put up with this. "You either trust me or you don't."

Reaching Southbank, Harrison stopped the car and reversed a little too fast into a car park on the road. He turned the ignition off but drummed the steering wheel with his fingers. "I don't know what to think, Zoe. Seems to me there's a connection between the two of you that's more than platonic."

"We've known each other for years, Harrison, that's all." Zoe struggled to remain calm. She could easily have let herself fall for Spencer's charms, but she hadn't. But how could she convince Harrison of that? Maybe it just wasn't going to work between them after all. Maybe this was God speaking to her, warning her. But somehow she struggled to believe that. Harrison was just insecure, but he had no need to be. That's all it was.

"I guess he'll be going to the funeral?"

Zoe shrugged. "I don't know. I didn't ask him, and he didn't say." She gave him a smile as she reached for his hand. "You're welcome to come, Harrison, you know that."

"I have to work."

Zoe released a breath. "Let's go to the restaurant. We can't sit here all night." She reached for the door handle.

Harrison pulled her back. "Zoe, look at me."

Zoe gulped as she turned and met his gaze. She'd never seen such a serious look on his face.

"Look me in the eye and tell me you don't love him."

She held his gaze for a moment before a chuckle burst out of her mouth. "Of course I don't love him. It's you I love, Harrison."

"But he has feelings for you."

107

"And if he does?" She angled her head, raising a brow.

"I don't want a showdown, Zoe. I need to be sure he's not going to lure you away."

She squeezed his hand and gazed into his eyes. "I won't let him, Harrison. Regardless of what he says." And that was the truth. She was attracted to Spencer, she couldn't deny that, and what they'd had as teenagers was special, but he'd broken his promise, and even if she was free to be with him, there'd always be that lingering thought he might do it again.

Leaning forward, she lifted her hand to Harrison's cheek and looked deeper into his eyes. "Harrison, I love you. I want to marry you. There isn't anyone else." Slipping her hand behind his neck, she drew his head closer to hers until their lips met in a kiss that left no doubt of her love and commitment.

When she pulled away, a playful grin sat on her face. "I don't mind having an argument if we make up like that all the time."

He held her gaze. His eyes had lightened and instead of fear and doubt and anger, she saw love. He smiled at her. "I'd rather not argue in the first place, Zoe."

She pulled him close again and hugged him. "Well, trust me."

He kissed the top of her head and then, tilting her head up, gazed into her eyes. "I'm sorry, Zoe. You had me worried." He brushed her cheek with his hand. "We'd best get our table."

"Sounds good. I'm famished." She reached up and popped another kiss on his lips before turning in her seat and reaching for the door handle again.

Before she could open the door, Harrison had jumped out and sprinted around to her side and opened it for her. A sense of well-being washed through her as he took her hand and interwove his fingers with hers.

After they ordered, Harrison reached out and took Zoe's hand as they sat at their table in the restaurant's alfresco area. Rubbing his thumb gently over her soft skin, he couldn't believe how close he'd come to losing her. He had no doubt Spencer still had his eyes on her. Harrison couldn't blame the guy—Zoe's beauty, especially tonight, dressed in her snugly fitting green dress, would cause any man's head to turn. And the way she'd pinned her hair, leaving a few strands trailing down her neck so they bounced seductively on her shoulders... he couldn't bear it if he lost her.

"It's lovely here, Harrison." Zoe's smile lit up her face, and he just wanted to pull her close and never let her go. But they were in public, even though their table was tucked away in a corner made private with potted plants and trailing semi-tropical vines.

"Yes, it is, but not as lovely as you."

Zoe laughed. "Harrison, stop it! You're just a big softie!"

"But it's true, Zoe. You're beautiful."

"Well, thank you. "A blush crept up her neck.

He squeezed her hand. "I'm sorry, Zoe. I shouldn't have doubted you."

"It's okay, Harrison. It's forgotten."

He gave her a wistful smile. "I just want us to be happy, but all we've done since we've been engaged is argue."

"Not quite true, but yes, it hasn't been quite the engagement I guess we were hoping for."

"I think that's an understatement." He lifted her hand and wove his fingers through hers.

"Well, I guess it's better to sort things out before we tie the knot."

"Which brings me to…"

"Harrison, no. We agreed." Zoe's voice was firm.

His heart fell. He'd been hoping she might have forgotten.

The waiter appeared with their meals—roast barramundi fillet with carrot, steamed broccolini and shrimp butter for her, and a roast rack of lamb with bacon, sweetbreads, peas and buttermilk for him. He placed them on the table and then held up a large pepper grinder. "Pepper for you, sir? Madam?" They both nodded and sat with their hands in their laps while the waiter ground the fine black seasoning on their meals. "Another drink, sir?"

Harrison glanced at Zoe and raised his brow.

She shook her head.

"No, thanks, we're all right for now."

After the waiter left, Zoe squeezed Harrison's hand. "Do you mind if we give thanks?"

Harrison stiffened slightly. This was something his parents did when they ate out, but he'd always thought it a little embarrassing to be seen bowing your head in public, but if it was something Zoe wanted to do, he guessed he'd go along with it to keep her happy. He shrugged. "Sure, why not?"

"I'll say it." She smiled at him before taking his hand and bowing her head. "Dear God, thank you for all the good things You give to us, especially this food. Please bless it to our bodies, Amen."

"Amen." Harrison lifted his head, relieved Zoe had kept it short.

"It wasn't so bad, was it?" Zoe's warm smile and knowing look made him laugh.

"No, it wasn't." He picked up his knife and fork, his mouth watering at the sight of the juicy rack of lamb on his plate. The smell of it had tantalised his taste buds since the waiter had brought it out.

"Harrison, there's something I'd like to ask you."

Slicing into the lamb, he placed a portion on his fork and looked up. "What's that?"

"Will you start coming to church with me?"

His eyes widened and he almost choked. *"Church?"*

Zoe nodded. "Yes, church. I think it'd be really good if we started going together."

He put his fork down and blew out a breath. He'd have to go along with it just to keep the peace, but maybe it wouldn't be such a bad thing to do, especially if it made Zoe happy. "Which one did you have in mind?"

"Your parents' church. I liked the pastor when we went at Christmas, and it seemed friendly enough. Your boss goes there too, doesn't she?"

"Yes… but she's leaving for Ecuador soon."

"That's a pity. I think I'd like to get to know her better." Zoe's brows were drawn as she took a sip of her lime and soda.

"They're only going for a few months." Picking up his fork, Harrison finally popped the lamb into his mouth. Definitely worth the wait. The best lamb he'd tasted in a long time.

"Okay, well, that's sorted then. As soon as I get back from the farm, we can start going."

Harrison gave a small chuckle. He wasn't quite sure how all of that had come about, but to be honest, if Zoe was happy, that's all that mattered.

Strolling along the boardwalk after dinner, Zoe leaned her head on Harrison's shoulder, warmth flowing through her as she thought about how the evening had turned out. Maybe God was working on Harrison's heart just like Mum had said He was. Agreeing to come to church was just a start, but it was good start, and gave her hope that in time they could grow together as Christians and that their marriage would be stronger because of their shared faith.

She lifted her face. "Are you sure you can't come for the funeral?"

Looking down, he brushed her hair with his hand. "I wish I could, but with Tessa finished, I've got to work. Sorry."

She sighed. She knew that, but it would have been good to have his support. "I'll miss you."

He kissed her head. "And I'll miss you, too."

Chapter Fourteen

The miles slipped away as Zoe drove back to the farm with Mum beside her in the passenger seat. The sense of loss lay heavily on both their hearts—it wasn't every day you lost your mother and grandmother. She tried not to think about Grandma's body being transported back to Bellhaven in a refrigerated vehicle. Whilst it was practical, there was no option if they were to bury her beside Grandfather, but the thought of Grandma lying in a refrigerated van made her sad. The only comfort was that it was just her body. Grandma, *the real Grandma*, was safe in the arms of Jesus.

"I'm going to miss her a lot, Mum." Zoe's gaze was fixed on the road ahead, but she struggled to hold her tears at bay.

"We all will, Zoe." Mum extended her hand and placed it gently on Zoe's leg. "Are you okay, sweetheart?"

Zoe dabbed her eyes with a tissue and nodded. "I will be."

"Zoe…" Mum leaned forward and stared out the windscreen. "Is that smoke?"

Zoe peered at the horizon. What had looked like a large grey cloud a little earlier was now a billowing, angry cloud of smoke. "Yes, and it's heading for Bellhaven."

Mum spoke quietly. "I need to call Dad." She pulled her phone out of her purse and flipped it open.

Zoe felt ill as she glanced at Mum holding the phone to her ear.

Mum shook her head. "No signal."

"Try mine." Zoe handed Mum her phone.

Mum shook her head again. "The same."

"I'll try the radio. See if we can get some news."

Switching on the radio, Zoe searched for the local station. She found it, but the signal was weak and with the crackle, she could hardly hear the news reader. She turned the volume up.

"A Watch and Act alert is in place for residents of Ridgewood, Lawnton and Bellhaven. All residents should prepare to evacuate. Unless the wind changes, these towns are right in the path of the fire. Next update will be in ten minutes."

Mum's face blanched. "What are we going to do, Zoe? I need to get home to Peter. He won't cope."

Zoe squeezed her hand. "Dad's with him, Mum. They'll be okay. I doubt we'll get through."

Mum glanced at Zoe, her face as white as a sheet, but then her gaze returned to the smoke cloud now covering the sun and looking more menacing by the second.

Flashing lights appeared in Zoe's rear view mirror. Moments later, a Fire and Rescue truck overtook them and sped off into the distance.

Zoe's throat grew dry as the pungent outside air began seeping in. Flicking the air intake switch to recycle, she grabbed her water bottle and took a large mouthful.

Up ahead a barrier blocked the road, and a sign pointed all traffic to the nearby town of Glenville.

"I wish we could contact Dad and Peter. I'm so worried about them..."

"We have to trust they'll be okay, Mum. We might get some news when we get to Glenville." Slowing, Zoe indicated right, but her gaze remained on the billowing cloud of smoke heading for Bellhaven. If the fire reached the farm, there'd be no chance of saving it. She let out a slow breath and tried to push down her growing concern. Over the years they'd had many fires threaten the area, but this one looked like it could be the worst. Her heart grew heavier. *God, would you please let the fire pass? And please keep Dad and Peter safe.* God was able to calm a storm and part the sea, and He could control the fire if He chose, but would He? *Your will, Your way, Your time, Lord. Please help me trust You, but I pray with all my heart You'll save the farm.*

Having turned right, Zoe planted her foot, and her little car responded. "Ten minutes, Mum, but keep checking for service."

Five minutes later, Mum let out a relieved sigh. "Finally." Holding her phone to her ear. Mum straightened in her seat. Seconds ticked by. "He's not answering, Zoe. It's gone to voice-mail." She sounded alarmed.

"Try again."

She did. Seconds later, she shook her head. "The same."

"He's probably busy. It doesn't mean anything." But despite Zoe's verbal assurances, concern over Dad and Peter kept growing. What if the fire had already reached the farm? What if they were in danger? She tried not to think about it and instead trust God to look after them, but images of burned buildings and charred bodies bombarded her mind. Her faith was really lacking if she was imagining things like that.

Another few minutes and they passed a sign telling them they were entering Glenville. It was the busiest she'd ever seen the small town. The main street was packed with cars, and people wearing worried faces scurried in all directions, but they mainly headed towards the community centre on Johnson Street.

Zoe reversed her Corolla into a small space between two large SUV's. She and Mum wasted no time in joining the throng of people heading to the centre. A registration table had been set up at the entrance of the building, and they joined the line. Apart from the sound of a few babies crying and a few mums calling out to their children to stop running around, a general hush filled the hall. It seemed everyone's thoughts were of their loved ones still in the line of fire, and on their homes. Were they still standing or had they been burned to the ground and were now just a charred heap?

Zoe was no different. She stood quietly with her arm around Mum as they inched slowly forward. Eventually it was their turn. As they stepped forward, a middle-aged woman with short, greying hair looked up, her eyes lighting up momentarily before filling with concern. "I didn't know you were back, Ruth. I was so sorry to hear about your mum."

The woman meant well, but her kind words made Mum's eyes fill with tears. "Thanks, Mary." Mum gave her an appreciative smile as she sniffed. "Zoe and I are on our way back to Bellhaven now." She paused, dabbing her eyes.

Zoe put her hand on Mum's back.

"You haven't seen Kevin and Peter, have you?" Mum struggled to get the words out.

Mary shook her head slowly. "I'm sorry, Ruth. They haven't come in yet."

Zoe gave Mum's shoulders a squeeze. *God, please look after them…*

"I'll let you know if I hear anything."

"Thank you." Mum gave another weak smile.

"There's tea, coffee and water to the side, and the folk from St Alban's are running a prayer vigil at the back. We're all praying no-one loses their life."

Especially Dad and Peter. A heavy weight settled on Zoe's heart as she led Mum towards the refreshments table. Surely Dad would return Mum's calls shortly. She'd left enough messages.

"I'm going to join the prayer group, Zoe," Mum said quietly as they stepped away from the desk.

"I'll come with you, just let me call Harrison first."

"Okay, sweetheart. Thank you." Mum squeezed Zoe's wrist, her hand shaking. "I wish he'd ring."

"I'll find out if anyone's seen them."

"Thanks." Mum smiled again, but Zoe could tell she was really struggling to hold herself together. Not knowing the whereabouts of your husband and son when an out of control fire was bearing down on your property would do that to you, even if you trusted God. How could anyone relax when they knew what devastation the fire could cause?

As Mum walked to the back of the room and joined the dozen or so people sitting in a circle with bowed heads, Zoe stepped outside and pulled her phone out. Harrison would be at work, but he'd answer if he could. Just about to press Harrison's number, Zoe's attention was drawn to the almost new Toyota Hilux pickup driving by. Her heart skipped a beat. How had Spencer gotten here so quickly? She slapped her forehead. *He has a plane...doh...* He pulled to a stop and his mother opened the door and climbed out. Mrs. Coleman lifted a hand in a small wave as he sped off.

Trudging along the pavement towards the centre, Mrs. Coleman hugged a small white dog to her chest, her focus obviously not on where she was going, because when she reached Zoe, she looked up with a start.

"Zoe... I didn't see you there." Her face was covered with fine black soot and her eyes were glassy.

"Are you all right, Mrs. Coleman?" Zoe placed her arm gently around Spencer's mum's shoulder. When she and Spencer were dating, Zoe had spent a lot of time at the Coleman's farm, and Mrs. Coleman was almost like a second mother to her.

Mrs. Coleman shook her head. "No...our...our house is gone."

Zoe's eyes widened. Had she heard correctly? The Coleman's house had been burned? That meant their's was next. Zoe forced herself to ignore her fears and turned her attention to Mrs. Coleman. "That's terrible, Mrs. Coleman. Let me help you inside." Zoe led Mrs. Coleman to a chair and quickly found a blanket to put around her shoulders. Shock was setting in. She organised a cup of sweet tea and sat beside her, rubbing her back gently to keep her warm. Despite the heat of the day, Mrs. Coleman was shivering.

"Is Mr. Coleman okay?" Zoe asked quietly, praying silently he was.

"I...I don't know. Spencer's gone back."

The dog whimpered. Mrs. Coleman tightened her grip on it.

Zoe wanted to ask which way the fire was heading, but refrained. She didn't have to. She knew. Instead, as she comforted Mrs. Coleman, she prayed silently. *God, please spare the farm and keep Dad and Peter safe, as well as Mr. Coleman and Spencer. I know You can answer prayer, so this would be a really good time to intervene. Please. I know You can. Please just keep them all safe.* She gulped. If only God would let her know He'd heard.

More people arrived, each wearing a tale of their own on their face. Zoe overhead snippets of information, none of it good. The fire's intensity was increasing. So far, three properties had been destroyed. No lives had been lost that they were aware of, but people were missing, and concern was held for their safety. Zoe gulped. How much more could these people endure? So many years of drought, and now everything they owned could be wiped out in an instant.

She felt so sorry for them. They all worked so hard. *So hard.* It wasn't fair. Why didn't God give them a break? They all just seemed to accept it as their lot in life. *"The Lord giveth and the Lord taketh away."* How many times had she heard that? She could get quite incensed about their simple acceptance, in fact, she was. *God, why don't You answer their prayers?*

Soft singing rose from the back of the hall. Everyone stopped their conversations and turned to face the group sitting in a circle at the back of the hall. They'd joined hands and were singing 'Great is Thy Faithfulness', unaccompanied. One by one, everyone in the hall joined in. Zoe whispered the words, and as she sang, something inside her softened and tears streamed down her cheeks. *"All I have needed Thy hand hath provided, Great is Thy faithfulness, Lord unto me."*

Silence filled the hall. Even those who normally wouldn't pray or sing stood quietly. Regardless of what was going on outside, God was here, working in people's hearts. God would provide, because He was faithful. Even if they lost their homes, He would provide. Zoe clutched her hands to her chest as a voice inside her said, *"Trust Me."*

Mrs. Coleman straightened. The vacant look in her eyes had disappeared and had been replaced with peace and calm. "That's all we can do, Zoe, trust the Lord and praise Him, regardless of the outcome."

She was right, but the fact Mrs. Coleman could say that after having just lost her home amazed Zoe. Especially when she didn't know if her husband and son were okay.

People soon returned to their conversations. Zoe remembered she'd promised Mum she'd try to find out about Dad, and she still hadn't called Harrison. She turned to Mrs. Coleman and placed her hand lightly on her back. "Will you be okay if I leave you for a few minutes?"

"Of course, dear. Thank you for being with me." She squeezed Zoe's hand, giving her a warm smile.

"I'll be back soon." Zoe stood and walked outside. She gagged on the air, thick with smoke and soot which was settling on the pavement and all the cars. The sky was a deep reddy-grey as the sun tried to penetrate the smoke. If it was this bad here, what was it like in the thick of it?

Zoe pulled her phone out again and dialled Harrison's number. He answered within three rings.

"Zoe, what's the matter?"

"You haven't heard?"

"Heard what?"

Leaning against the wall, Zoe closed her eyes momentarily and lifted a hand to her face. "It's horrible, Harrison. There's an out of control bush-fire heading for the farm. It's already been through the Coleman's farm and two others and destroyed everything." She struggled to get the words out.

"Zoe, that's terrible. Are you okay?"

"Yes." She gulped. "But we're not sure about Dad and Peter."

"Where are they?"

She blew out a slow breath as those words played in her mind… 'Trust me'. "We don't know. I'm just about to ask around."

"I'll come out."

Tears pricked Zoe's eyes. She could really do with Harrison's arms around her right now. "Would you?" Her voice was tiny.

"Yes. I'll leave straight away."

"Thank you. Be careful." She gulped again. "I love you."

"I love you, too, Zoe. Hang in there."

"I will."

Zoe ended the call and looked at the sky, covering her mouth and nose with her hand. The smoky air was stinging her nostrils and her throat was really dry. But she had another call to make. The Transport company. They couldn't bring Grandma's body out here with a fire raging. What if the Funeral Home burned down? She stepped into the entrance away from the smoke and made the call.

Next, Zoe needed to find someone who might know about Dad. Inside the hall, an information desk was being set up. She caught Mum's eye and motioned for her to come. Mum stood and hurried to join her. They joined the line of people who seemed just as keen to obtain information as they were.

An older bald headed man wearing a Rural Fire Services uniform looked up when it was their turn. "Hello. How can I help?"

"Do you have any information on Bellrae, Kevin Taylor's farm over near Bellhaven?"

While the man looked down at his computer, Zoe's heart pounded and her grip on Mum's shoulder tightened. They had to be okay.

Finally, the man lifted his head. "The property's still in danger, and there's a crew on their way out there. The report says the owner went back to look for his son instead of leaving. That's all I've got. I'm sorry."

Zoe's heart felt as if it had been ripped from her chest. *Of course Dad would go back for Peter.* Somehow she thanked the man and led Mum to the seat beside Mrs. Coleman. As she sat, she once again heard those words… *'Trust Me'.*

Peter huddled in the hay with his arms wrapped around his favourite red hen, Ginger. He had to protect her from the horrible black monster in the sky. She'd be scared of it. Just like Chicken Little, she'd be thinking the world was about to end. *Maybe it was.* Peter huddled further into the hay. If the monster couldn't see them, they'd be all right.

Chapter Fifteen

Never had five hours taken so long. Harrison prayed, yes, he prayed, that his car would behave. If God had any power, this was the time to prove it. Zoe needed him, and he had to get to her. No doubt Spencer would be there too, and the last thing Harrison wanted was for Spencer to be the hero again.

As the hours ticked by, the sky grew darker, the sun a fierce ball of red trying to penetrate a thickening blanket of smoke. Harrison switched his headlights on as he passed through Arlington. Glancing at Joe's Mechanical Repairs, he thanked God he didn't need to stop.

He did call Zoe, however, while he had a signal.

"We're still at the Community Centre at Glenville, Harrison."

"I'll be there soon, Zo. Have your Dad and Peter been found yet?"

Zoe's voice caught. "No, they're still missing."

"What about the fire?"

"It's slowed a little, but it's still burning and heading for Bellrae."

"I'm praying for you all, Zo." The words slipped out of his mouth. Had he really said that?

"Thank you, Harrison." Her voice caught again. "Drive carefully."

Before he could answer, his phone beeped, ending the call. The signal was lost. Leaving the town, he put his foot down.

Kevin Taylor jumped out of his old pickup, lifting his shirt to cover his face, and scanned the fence-line. He could barely see more than a few metres either side, the smoke so thick he could almost cut it with a knife. He was starting to panic. Where had Peter gone? He'd already scoured all the places he could think of, but the property was so big, he couldn't search it all. Besides, Peter couldn't have gone that far. But it was like finding a needle in a haystack. Why hadn't he just stayed put when he'd been told? Kevin raked his hand across his balding head. *Silly boy.* It was no use. He'd never find him. But would Ruth ever forgive him if something happened to Peter?

Kevin peered through the smoke-thickened air once more before jumping back into the pickup. He'd just have to go back to the house and pray Peter had returned. If he could get there, that is. Tongues of fire licked the dry grass at the fence-line. How could a fire spread so easily when the cattle struggled to find enough grass to eat?

He gunned it as he headed back along the fence-line to the track leading back to the farm. He hit the brakes—a wall of fire was in his path. Swinging off the track, he headed across the paddock away from it. Kevin gripped the steering wheel as the pickup bounced across the rough ground. He should slow down, but a glance in the rear view mirror told him how foolish that would be. The fire was gaining ground. He floored it. He had to get out of there. It'd been foolish to come out on his own. What was he thinking? As he struggled to retain control, the pickup hit a ditch and rolled.

Zoe sat with Mum and Mrs. Coleman and waited. As every minute passed, hope of finding Dad and Peter alive diminished. As she sat, Zoe prayed. What else could she do? Go and look for them herself? She would if she could, but Mum needed her. Every now and again they looked up as someone new entered the hall. But no-one had any news about the whereabouts of Kevin and Peter Taylor. At least Uncle Stephen and Aunt Veronica were safe. They'd gone to Melbourne to visit family.

Spencer and Mr. Coleman were helping fight the fire with the volunteer fire brigade, Spencer flying an agricultural plane adapted for fire-fighting purposes, dumping water drawn from the Ridgewood dam onto the fire, and Mr. Coleman was helping on the ground. The three women prayed for their safety.

Fire fighters had arrived from interstate to help fight the blaze, and Zoe had heard reports it was being contained.

"We have to hear something soon, Zoe." Mum was trying to be positive and not to worry, but every few minutes she'd check her phone.

Zoe reached over and squeezed Mum's hand. She prayed the news would be good when it came. What would they do if…no, she couldn't go there. No good would come from dwelling on that possibility.

Ladies from the local branch of the Country Women's Association handed sandwiches around. Zoe took a bite of a ham and tomato sandwich but could barely swallow it. She felt sick in her stomach. The three women rejoined the prayer group. More than twenty people sat in groups of four and five and prayed together for the safety of those fighting the fire and those still missing.

As Zoe listened to the prayers of those around her, especially Mrs. Coleman's, a strange feeling stirred within her. Although everyone clung to the promises God had given in the Bible that He'd care for them in times of trouble, what spoke to her the most was the commitment that regardless of the outcome, they'd still trust God, *because He was God*. He was the Alpha and Omega, the Beginning and the End, the great Jehovah. Like the men of old, their lives were in His hand.

Zoe swallowed hard. It had been a long time since she'd prayed in a group, but her heart quickened and she knew she needed to. Being a by-stander wasn't good enough. When there was a pause, she cleared her throat. "Lord God, I'm not sure what more I can add, I feel so inadequate." She drew a breath. "I ask you keep the men safe, especially my dad and brother. But Lord, help me to also trust You. You know I struggle with that, because I often take my eyes off You and don't see the bigger picture. Perhaps my prayers are too selfish, but Lord God, if at all possible, would You please save them?" Her voice caught, and she paused before continuing. "I'm starting to understand that it's not so much what happens to us that's important, it's how we handle it. Thank you for these faithful people who've helped show me the way. Please help me to trust You, regardless of what happens. Amen." Zoe wiped her eyes and drew another breath. As she opened her eyes, a warm hand rested on her shoulder. Without looking, she knew it was Harrison.

Lifting her hand, she placed it on top of his and squeezed it. How much of her prayer had he heard? She'd never expected him to hear it, but maybe God could use her honesty and vulnerability to soften his heart.

After a few moments, Zoe stood quietly and stepped into Harrison's arms. She clung to him as he kissed the top of her hair and rubbed her back. She felt safe in his arms, and unbidden tears welled up inside her.

"Let's take a walk, Zoe," he whispered into her ear.

Nodding, she walked with him to the entrance, but the air was too thick with smoke, so they moved back inside and found a quiet spot in the hall. He turned her to face him, and tilting her chin up with his finger, looked at her with his deep brown eyes. "I stopped to speak with a man on the way here. Turned out it was Spencer's father."

Harrison's serious expression gave her the feeling he was about to break some bad news. Remembering her prayer, she steeled herself, but a hard lump formed in her throat. If this was a test, she wanted to pass it, but she couldn't stop the feeling of dread clawing at her.

"Spencer thinks he saw your father driving his pickup out near the fire."

Zoe's eyes widened. *What was Dad doing there?*

"He's not sure, but he said it looked like him."

Zoe opened her mouth to speak. Harrison placed his finger over it. "They don't know. Nobody's gone out looking yet because they're still trying to contain the fire."

Zoe drew a slow breath. "I should tell Mum."

"Yes, but you can also tell her the farm's safe for the moment."

A small amount of relief flowed through Zoe, but until Dad and Peter were both safe as well, the farm really didn't matter.

"Let's tell her." She took his hand and together they walked towards the prayer circle. Zoe tapped Mum on the shoulder.

Mum lifted her head, her eyes widening. "Is there news?" She spoke softly but urgently, almost mouthing the words.

Zoe nodded and motioned with her head for Mum to move away from the group.

Mum pushed her chair back quietly and stepped with them to an empty spot close by. "Is it good or bad?" Mum looked up with uneasiness in her eyes.

Zoe squeezed her hand. "Mainly good." She told Mum what she knew. While Mum was relieved to hear the farm was safe, like Zoe, her main concern was for Dad and Peter. "I just need to know they're safe." Tears welled in her eyes.

"I know, Mum. Hopefully we'll hear soon."

"I'm sorry, Mrs. Taylor. They couldn't tell me anything else." Harrison spoke with compassion as he rubbed her arm. "I said I'd go back and help, so I'll let you know as soon as I hear anything."

"Thank you, Harrison." Mum gave a weak smile as she looked up at him. "Take care out there… it's dangerous."

"I will. They won't let me go near the containment line— I'm just going back with some supplies. I'll be back as soon as I can…hopefully with Kevin and Peter."

"I'm coming with you, Harrison." Zoe grabbed his arm.

Harrison's eyes sprung open. "No, Zoe. Stay here with your mum."

She held his gaze. "I need to do something, Harrison. I can't sit around here any longer." Her voice softened. "Mum will be okay."

His gaze didn't flinch. "It's not pretty out there, Zoe."

"I don't care. I'm coming."

Harrison raised his brow but remained silent.

Zoe turned, and taking Mum's wrist in her hand, softened her tone. "I'm going to find Dad and Peter, Mum. I'll be okay, don't you worry."

Mum's eyes moistened. "Be careful, Zoe."

She leaned down and gave Mum a kiss on the cheek. "I will." She then turned, and linking her arm through Harrison's, strode to the front of the hall and out the door.

"You do look very attractive when you're wound up, Zoe." If the situation wasn't so serious, she would have laughed at the grin on Harrison's face, but instead, she just gave him a firm glare. This wasn't the time or the place for frivolity.

Harrison headed towards Mr. Coleman's pickup.

"Where's your car?" Zoe asked as she climbed into the passenger seat.

"Swapped it for this to bring back the supplies." Harrison turned the key and pulled away from the gutter.

Zoe glanced in the back. Barrels of water and protective clothing filled the cabin. A sense of pride welled up within her as she glanced at Harrison and she smiled to herself. He didn't have to help, but the fact that he was, warmed her heart.

Her smile soon slipped. The charred ground, still smouldering and sparking, looked like a war zone. Passing the entrance to the Coleman's farm, Zoe's gaze settled on the glowing mound on the hill. She swallowed the bile that rose in her throat. How could it have happened so quickly? She reached for Harrison's hand.

The fire had moved to the right and was slowly moving towards the next farm. For now, Bellrae was spared. Zoe held her hand to her chest, and letting out a relieved breath, sent up a silent prayer of thanks.

Harrison slowed the Hilux as they approached the command station.

Zoe scanned the area. No sign of Dad or Peter. Just a group of volunteer fire-fighters, including Mr. Coleman, standing around in a circle studying a map.

"Best stay in the car, Zoe." Harrison gave her a firm look as he squeezed her hand.

Her shoulders slumped, but he was right. This was a man's domain, even if she was more than capable of helping.

Harrison climbed down and lifted the supplies out of the back. He spent a few minutes with the men, and climbed back in.

"Any word on Dad and Peter?" Zoe peered into his eyes.

"No, but a search vehicle's gone looking for them."

"I want to look too."

He gave a small chuckle. "Thought you might."

"Let me drive."

Angling his head, Harrison raised a brow.

"I know the farm like the back of my hand."

"Okay, we'll swap when we get to your place."

Leaning forward, Zoe peered through the smoke, but having learned to drive in these very paddocks, she knew almost every dip and hollow. But where would Dad be? The top paddock? Or maybe the lower one? "Did they give any idea where he was?" Zoe glanced quickly at Harrison, his body taut as he held onto the grab handle with both hands.

"No, they just mentioned a fence line, that's all."

Zoe yanked the steering wheel to the left and planted her foot. The Hilux picked up speed as she pointed it towards the red glow in the distance. Finding the rough track she and Spencer used to ride their quad bikes on, she told her mind not to go there. She had to find Dad, and to do that, she had to focus. As the smoke grew thicker, she slowed down, the headlights barely penetrating the thick swirling mass in the growing darkness of the night.

"We should turn back, Zoe."

She glanced at him. "We can't leave them out here."

"It's too dangerous."

"I'm not stopping, Harrison. I can't leave them out here to die."

"We should leave it to the search team. What if we get caught in the fire?"

"We won't."

"How can you be so sure?"

She had no answer. But she'd made a promise to Mum, and she was going to keep it. Gritting her teeth, she prayed God would protect them and lead them to Dad and Peter.

Chapter Sixteen

Kevin moaned. His leg hurt like nobody's business. Jammed under the dashboard, no way was it budging. But worse still, the cabin of the truck was thick with smoke and he could barely breathe. He covered his face with his shirt—he had to stay calm. *Please send someone, God. Please.*

He drifted in and out of consciousness. Sometime later, above the sound of crackling undergrowth, he heard the rumble of a vehicle. And then a voice. Someone had come. Tears pricked his eyes.

"Dad! Dad! I'm here. Are you all right?"

Tears streamed down his face as relief filled his heart. Zoe had come for him. He was going to live.

"Dad, we're going to get you out of there. Stay with us, okay?" Zoe reached out to him through the smashed windscreen. She felt his pulse. Weak, but still breathing. She grabbed her water bottle and squeezed a few drops of water into his mouth as her eyes searched around the cab. Her heart fell. Peter wasn't there. "Dad, where's Peter?"

Dad moaned.

Harrison joined her, poking his head through the gap where the windscreen should have been.

Zoe glanced at him. "Peter's not here, but Dad's breathing. We've got to get him out."

"How are we going to do that?"

Zoe gulped. She had no idea. The truck was lying at an awkward angle, the driver's door jammed into the ground, and Dad appeared to be wedged between the steering wheel and the seat. The only way out was through the front, but how could they do that without knowing what injuries he had? Zoe had no idea, but they had to take the risk. If they didn't get him out, he could burn to death.

"Climb in and try to manoeuvre him out of the seat, and I'll help drag him out. Be careful with his leg."

"I'll try. It's going to be tricky."

Zoe met Harrison's gaze. "I know, but what else can we do?"

Harrison shrugged before picking his way through the glass and into the cab. The awkward angle made it difficult for him to get a footing, but he wedged himself between the dashboard and the passenger seat. He tried to lift Dad out.

Dad screamed, his eyes opening wide, reflecting the pain he was in. "My leg..."

Zoe quickly met Harrison's gaze again. It wasn't good.

"I'll see if I can free it." Harrison balanced precariously as he reached down Dad's leg. He looked back at Zoe. "It's wedged under the pedal."

"Can you free it?" Zoe climbed in as far as she could.

Harrison panted. "Maybe."

Dad let out a blood curdling yell.

Zoe held her breath. Seconds passed.

Harrison's head bobbed back up. "Got it."

Zoe released her breath. His leg must be broken, but what could they do? "Okay, lift him up and I'll help drag him through. Dad, can you hear me?"

Moaning, Dad gave a small nod.

"This will hurt, but hang in there, okay?"

"Okay." His voice was a ragged whisper.

Inch by inch, Harrison raised him up. The pain-filled groans coming from deep within Dad tore at Zoe's heartstrings, but they couldn't stop. Better to suffer short term pain than become fuel for the fire. Zoe ignored the pain in her own body as she took Dad's weight from Harrison and waited for him to climb out and help her lower Dad to the ground, all the while trying to support his lower leg.

Finally, they laid Dad on the ground. Zoe grabbed her water again and squirted several more drops into his mouth as she wiped away blood from his blackened forehead with a strip she tore from her shirt. She leaned over him. "Do you know where Peter is, Dad?"

His breaths came fast, and he coughed as he tried to speak. He shook his head.

Panic set in. *Where was he?*

They couldn't stay to look—they had to get away from the smoke, and soon. What damage was it doing to them all? She took a quick look at Dad's leg. No wonder he was screaming in agony. His foot sat at an odd angle.

"Let's get him into the back. We'll need to lift him carefully."

Harrison leaned down, and together they picked him up and placed him as gently as they could onto the back of the pickup.

"I'll sit with him while you drive. Best head straight to Glenville."

Harrison raised his brow. "Hope I don't get lost."

"It's that way." Zoe pointed through the smoke back the way they'd come.

"Right. It's clear as mud. Or should I say, smoke?"

"No time for jokes, Harrison." Her eyes met his brown ones.

"Sorry." He dipped his head, and opening the door, climbed in.

Zoe cradled Dad's head on her lap and prayed Harrison would drive carefully—no more ditches, please. As the pickup bounced along at a slow pace, her eyes peered through the growing darkness at the blackened paddock and the swirling smoke tinged with red. Where was Peter? She took some deep breaths. *Lord God, please help us find him. You know where he is. Please be with him and lead us to him. Please help him not to be scared.*

The farmhouse was in darkness when they passed by. Zoe shivered at the eerie sight. Normally the security lights would be on, but she guessed all power had been cut. They continued on, and soon after passing the house, Harrison turned onto the road to Glenville. Zoe kept wiping Dad's face but couldn't do anything about his pain. His groans grew louder with every passing minute.

The main street of Glenville was still filled with vehicles from the surrounding area. When Harrison double-parked in front of the Community Centre, Zoe, stiff and sore from sitting in one spot for so long, could barely move. Harrison reached in and helped ease Dad off her, and just as she was moving to help lift him down, a voice called out.

"Zoe, we were all worried about you."

She lifted her head. To her annoyance, her heart skipped a beat. Spencer was striding towards the truck. When would her heart listen to her head? She wasn't interested in Spencer Coleman anymore. She glanced at Harrison to gauge his reaction. His jaw was clenched.

"Where've you been?" Spencer almost sounded angry.

"Looking for Dad. We found him."

"There was already a search party out looking for him."

"I couldn't wait, sorry. Anyway, we found him, but Peter's still missing."

Spencer's face blanched. "He wasn't with your dad?"

Zoe shook her head as she carefully helped lift Dad to the back of the truck. She didn't trust herself to speak.

"Any idea where he might be?" Spencer asked as he and Harrison lifted Dad onto the pavement.

She shrugged. "He'll be hiding somewhere, and he'll be scared. I'd go, but I have to look after Dad." She climbed down onto the ground.

"I'll go, Zoe." Harrison said.

"I'll go with you." Spencer added.

Zoe raised her brow. "Okay. Check if his quad bike's gone. If it's not, good chance he's hiding around the farmhouse."

"We'll bring him back, Zoe." Harrison placed his hand on her shoulder as they crouched around Dad.

She lifted her face and her eyes met his—such determination she'd not seen before. Harrison had a purpose. Maybe he wanted to prove he could match Spencer's heroism. There was no need. He was her hero, he didn't need to prove it.

"Thanks." She gave him a grateful smile before he and Spencer strode off.

Zoe bent down on one knee and inspected Dad's ankle. It was a mess, but he was alive.

"Not looking good." An older voice that seemed vaguely familiar sounded above her.

She looked up—it was Spencer's grandfather, and he was crouching beside her.

"No, he's in a lot of pain."

"Let's get him inside. I'll grab a stretcher." Mr. Coleman senior disappeared inside and returned a few minutes later with a stretcher and several helpers. *And Mum.*

As Mum raced past the men, tears streamed down her face. She knelt down and cradled his head, showering kisses all over his face.

Zoe pushed back tears of her own. Never had she seen her mother be so open with her love for Dad.

"Where did you find him?" Lifting her head, Mum wiped her face with the back of her hand.

"In the back paddock."

"Peter?" She sounded desperate.

Zoe gulped and took a deep breath. "Harrison and Spencer have gone back to look for him."

Mum's gaze remained steady. "Let's pray they find him."

"I'm sure they will." But she wasn't sure at all—how could she be? But she prayed with all her heart he'd be found, safe and unharmed.

The men lifted Dad onto the stretcher and carried him inside, placing the stretcher in a corner where a temporary Triage centre had been set up. No doctors, just two nurses and one paramedic. A doctor was on his way, so they'd been told.

Zoe drew a breath. This is what she'd spent the last five years studying for. She may not have officially started her Internship yet, but she knew what to do.

"This is my dad, and I'm a trained doctor. Can you help me with him?" Zoe looked at the nurse who stood beside her.

"Sure, what do you need?"

"Ice, and something to splint his leg with, and some pain relief."

"I'll be right back."

Carefully loosening Dad's laces, Zoe felt his lower leg. Dad winced. She glanced at him. "I'm sorry, Dad, I've got to do this."

Zoe continued inspecting his leg while she waited. Mum stood beside Dad, holding his hand. His ankle was swollen, and although there were no protruding bones, the lump just

136

above his ankle suggested he'd broken his tibia. No blood, thankfully.

"I'm so glad you found him, Zoe." Mum sounded relieved.

"So am I, Mum. He'll be okay—he'll need surgery, but he'll be okay."

The nurse arrived back with an ice pack, aspirin, two flat boards she'd found somewhere, and a crepe bandage. Zoe smiled at her. "You did well."

The nurse's face lit up. She obviously wasn't used to praise.

With the nurse's help, Zoe applied the ice pack and positioned the boards either side of Dad's leg, and then wrapped it carefully with the bandage. Basic first aid, but it felt good knowing what to do. "How's that feel, Dad?"

"Still sore, but better." His lips parted slightly, as if he were attempting a smile.

"We'll get you to hospital as soon as we can." Zoe raised her head and looked at the nurse. "Any ambulances available?"

The nurse shook her head. "Still waiting for one to return."

"How long?"

She shrugged. "Another half hour? It's a two-hour round trip to Blackwell."

Zoe knew that all too well. The locals had been lobbying for a hospital of their own for years, but it had never eventuated. She smoothed the hair off Dad's forehead. Could he wait that long? The pain in his face had lessened a little, but she didn't like his colour, nor the way he was coughing and wheezing. Zoe's heart fell. She'd been so focused on getting Dad away from the fire and stabilising his leg she'd overlooked the damage he might have suffered from inhaling all that smoke. He'd survive a broken leg, but he mightn't survive smoke inhalation. She grimaced. *How stupid!* Leaning over, she listened to his chest. His breathing was irregular. She took a closer inspection of his mouth and nose. No visible burns. "Dad, have you got any pain in your chest?" She searched his face as she brushed his forehead.

He pressed his hand to his chest as he coughed again and shook his head.

Zoe breathed a sigh of relief. But still, he needed proper attention, more than what they could give him here. She looked up at the nurse. "Can you check on that ambulance?"

She nodded and then scooted away. Within minutes she returned. "It'll be here in less than ten minutes."

"Great. No-one else is waiting for it?"

"Not that I'm aware of."

Zoe turned to Mum. "Do you want to go with Dad or stay here and wait for news on Peter?"

"Oh Zoe, I don't know." She looked down at Dad and squeezed his hand. "I don't know."

"Go with Dad and I'll call as soon as we hear anything."

"I'll come with you, Ruth." Mrs. Coleman stood behind Mum, her hand resting on Mum's shoulder.

Instant relief showed on Mum's face. "Would you, Hilda?"

"Of course, Ruth. You need a friend with you."

Mum's eyes moistened. "Thank you." Mum turned her gaze to Zoe. "Let me know when they find Peter."

"I will, Mum, don't you worry. I'm sure they'll find him soon." But she still had no way of knowing that. A sudden image of Harrison and Spencer working together flashed through Zoe's mind. If the circumstances had been different, she would have smiled.

Harrison glanced at the man sitting beside him in the driver's seat. Never had he expected to be in the same car as Spencer Coleman, yet here they were, together and alone, speeding along a country road in the dark, on a mission to find Zoe's brother. At any other time and for any other reason, this just wouldn't have happened, but they needed to find Peter. Harrison found himself praying again. Strange, because he didn't really believe God would bother listening to him, given they had zero relationship, but it seemed the only thing he could do, and he did it without thinking. They really needed to find Peter alive and well. The alternative just wasn't thinkable. And besides, he wanted to do it for Zoe. *God, if You can hear me, please help us to find Peter alive and well. Show us where he is. Thank you.*

Harrison held on as Spencer braked harshly before turning into the entrance to Bellrae. The glow in the sky had lessened in the half hour or so since he and Zoe had driven down here with Kevin in the back, but the air, still thick with smoke, burned his nostrils and made visibility low.

Spencer flicked a switch and the whole area around them lit up.

"Wow. How many lights have you got?"

Spencer chuckled. "A few."

Although the light bounced off the smoke, they could still see a whole lot better than before.

"Any idea where he might be?" Harrison asked as he peered out.

"Got a couple of ideas. We used to play hide and seek with Peter, and he had his favourite spots."

Harrison fought back the jealousy rising in his chest. Spencer and the Taylor kids had known each other a long time—he had no right to feel envious of the times they'd played together. "How long have you known Zoe?"

139

Spencer chuckled. "Just about as long as I can remember. She's a good one, Harrison...look after her."

Harrison's eyes kept searching the dark for Peter. "I will, no two ways about that."

"She loves you."

Harrison's eyes widened as he turned his head and met Spencer's gaze. He could hardly believe he was hearing those words come out of Spencer's mouth.

"I mean it...she really does love you. You don't need to worry about me."

Harrison blinked. How had Spencer known?

Spencer grimaced before returning his focus to the front. "I was foolish and lost her. My mistake."

Harrison cocked a brow, a sympathetic, but relieved grin tugging at the corner of his mouth. "Your loss, my gain."

"You could say that." Spencer drew a breath. "Anyway, I've been thinking...I reckon Peter could be in one of two places." He pulled up in front of the darkened farmhouse but left the truck running and the spotlights on. "There's a tree house round the back, and there's the barn—both places he's been known to hide in for hours."

"Right, I'll follow you."

Harrison caught the flashlight Spencer tossed him and flicked it on. Coughing, he covered his mouth with his arm and prayed Peter was still conscious but he feared the worst. How could anyone survive this?

He followed Spencer around the back to the tree house. An image of Spencer chasing a laughing Zoe up the ladder flashed through his mind. He gulped. *Focus on finding Peter.*

Spencer climbed the ladder and poked his head in.

"Can you see him?"

Climbing back down, Spencer shook his head and raked his hand through his hair. "He has to be in the barn."

"Let's hope so." Harrison followed Spencer to the barn on the other side of the farmhouse.

The door was open, and they flashed their lights around. An old rusty tractor sat in the entrance. Behind it lay bundles of hay. One was open, and something about it made them take a closer look. Was there a sound? A hen clucking? Not an unusual sound for a farm, but none were visible.

They ran forward, and leaning over the railing, raked through the loose hay. Spencer pulled out a red hen which squawked loudly in his hands. He let it go on the ground.

Harrison rummaged deeper into the hay. His hand froze at the touch of a body. *Peter.* "He's here! Under the hay." Harrison jumped over the railing and dug further until Peter's body was in the open. He cleared Peter's nose and mouth and placed his ear against Peter's chest. "He's alive, but only just."

Spencer jumped over the railing, and together they lifted him back over and onto the ground, pulling his head slightly back. "Peter, can you hear me?" Harrison did two chest compressions.

Peter's eyes sprung open and he coughed.

Harrison sighed with relief.

"Good job, mate." Spencer slapped him on the back. "You found him."

"Ginger? Where's Ginger?" Peter's voice was hoarse and he coughed again.

"The chicken?" Spencer asked.

"Yes, Ginger, my chicken. The monster was coming for her."

"She's fine, Peter, and so are you. The monster's gone away. Come on, let's get you out of here."

Spencer lifted him up and carried him to the truck, placing him in the middle of the seat and giving him a drink of water.

"Grandma's not coming back. Grandma's dead." Peter coughed as he squeezed the water into his mouth.

"It's very sad, Peter," Spencer said. "But she's gone to heaven."

"Grandma's gone to heaven. She's with God."

"That's right. She's with God."

As Harrison listened to the conversation between the two, he warmed to Spencer. He cared about Peter, he really did. He wasn't putting it on. Seems he wasn't a bad sort after all.

Chapter Seventeen

Zoe's phone buzzed. Her heart thumped. *Harrison...* Had they found Peter, and if so, was he alive? Her chest heaved as she tapped the green flashing phone icon. "Harrison—have you found him?" She held her breath.

"Yes, we've found him, Zoe. He's fine."

Zoe's hand flew to her chest and tears streamed down her cheeks. "Where was he?"

"Hiding in the barn."

Zoe let out a small chuckle. "Of course he was. Under some hay?"

"Yep."

Zoe shook her head. "I should have thought of that."

"It doesn't matter, Spencer did."

Was she hearing right? Harrison was promoting Spencer? *Unbelievable.* "I need to call Mum. She's on her way to the hospital with Dad."

"I'll see you soon. I love you, Zoe."

She smiled. "I love you too, Harrison."

Zoe called Mum straight away and gave her the good news. Mum was so relieved. That meant everyone was accounted for. No lives had been lost, although four farmhouses, including the Coleman's, had been destroyed, along with several hundred head of cattle and thousands of acres of farm land. She felt so bad for the Coleman's. Like her parents, Mr. and Mrs. Coleman had worked so hard, and now they'd lost everything. Could they rebuild and start again? *Would they want to?*

Zoe let out a sigh as she walked outside and waited for Harrison, Spencer and Peter to arrive. The glow from the fire still lit up the night sky, but at least the air had cleared a little. The fire fighters were still out there trying to gain the upper hand in the cool of the evening before another hot day dawned. No-one would be going home tonight, but tomorrow they'd get to see the full extent of the damage.

Headlights appeared in the distance and drew closer. Spencer's truck pulled up in front of her and Harrison climbed out, followed by Peter. She drew both of them into her arms and hugged them tight.

"Zoe, you're hurting me." Peter said.

She laughed. "I'm sorry, Peter, I was just glad to see you."

"The monster's gone, Zoe. Ginger's safe, and Grandma's in heaven."

She smiled over Peter's head and met Harrison's gaze, her heart warming at the look of him. Pieces of straw stuck in his beard and his hair, and his face was smudged with soot, but she'd never seen him look more handsome. The rugged look really suited him.

Once Peter was cleaned, fed, and settled on one of the makeshift beds, Zoe slipped her arm around Harrison's waist. "Come for a walk?"

"I've been waiting to be alone with you, Zoe." His hand rested on her shoulder as they headed for the door.

After the heat of the day, the cool night air, although still laced with smoke, was fresh on Zoe's face. They walked along the pavement, arm in arm, past all the closed, empty stores until they reached open space. The moon was blood red and looked larger than normal as wispy grey clouds drifted around it.

They reached the bridge crossing the Glen River, just a dry river bed waiting for water to fill it so it could flow again. Stopping in the middle, they leaned on the railing and looked down onto the sand below. Somewhere in the distance a dingo howled, but closer, raucous grunts of nesting bush turkeys reached their ears.

"Thanks for coming out, Harrison," Zoe said quietly.

"I'm glad I came." He traced her hairline with his finger and turned her to face him. "And I'm glad we found your dad and Peter." He held her gaze.

"I was so relieved." Her pulse quickened as he cupped her cheeks in his hands.

"I love you, Zoe."

She smiled up at him as she pulled another piece of hay from his hair. "I love you too, Harrison."

He lowered his face and kissed her gently.

The following morning, the buzz in the hall grew as the fifty or so people who'd slept on the floor began to stir. Zoe reached out and touched Harrison's cheek. "Hey."

His eyes opened. "Hey yourself." His eyes sparkled as he pulled her close and stroked her hair.

Zoe stifled a giggle. "Harrison, not here."

"I don't see why not." A smile grew on his face. "I look forward to waking up with you every morning, Zoe."

Zoe drew a breath and let it out slowly. Waking up with Harrison every morning would be wonderful, but she still couldn't bring herself to set a date. Not yet. She gave him a winsome smile. "You'll just have to have patience a while longer."

His lip came out in a pout as disappointment filled his face.

"Are you two going to kiss?" Peter appeared beside them.

Zoe chuckled. Trust Peter to come to the rescue. "No, not here, Peter." Pulling herself up, she slipped her arm around Peter's shoulder. "How are you feeling this morning?"

"I've never had a sleep-over with this many people." His eyes sparkled.

"Neither have we." Zoe chuckled again. "Have you seen Mum?"

"She's over there with Mrs. Coleman. She gave me breakfast."

Zoe's gaze shifted to the tables sitting against the side of the hall where Mum and Mrs. Coleman were helping serve breakfast. She shook her head. How could they do that after getting back so late from the hospital? They were both hard working and generous women, but the love and care they were showing others in the midst of their own grief challenged Zoe. It wasn't all about them and what they'd lost. It was about what they could give. She could learn a lot from them.

The day passed in a hive of activity. A trip to the hospital to see Dad. He was being treated for smoke inhalation, but had to wait until the swelling went down in his leg before his ankle could be operated on. He'd be out of action for some time. Zoe, Harrison, Mum and Peter went with the Coleman's to inspect the charred remains of their home and property. Tears streamed down Mrs. Coleman's face as they sifted through the rubble, occasionally finding an item that somehow hadn't been burned, but they were few and far between.

"I'm so sorry." Zoe wrapped her arms around Mrs. Coleman without thinking. Her heart went out to this family who'd lost everything.

"It's okay, dear. We can rebuild, and we still have each other. That's the main thing." She wiped her eyes. "God will provide for us."

Zoe gulped. How could she be so positive about it all? "But where will you stay in the meantime? And how will you survive?"

"I don't know yet, Zoe, but I'm sure He'll look after us."

"Maybe you could stay in Grandma's cottage." Zoe choked on her words. They hadn't even buried her yet.

Mrs. Coleman pulled back and dabbed her eyes. "Zoe, what a lovely thought, but you'd better check with your mum about that."

"I don't think she'll mind, in fact, I think she'll be more than happy." Zoe gave Mrs. Coleman a warm smile as Mum appeared beside them. "And here she is now." Zoe turned to face Mum and placed her arm around her shoulder. "What do you think of the Coleman's staying in Grandma's cottage?"

Mum's eyes lit up. "Of course they can. I should have thought of it myself."

"Shall we start cleaning it out?" Zoe asked.

"It has to be done, so now's as good a time as any." Mum turned to Mrs. Coleman and took her hands. "You'll have a bed to sleep in tonight, Hilda."

Tears ran down Mrs. Coleman's cheeks. "Thank you, Ruth. It's so kind of you."

Zoe, Mum and Mrs. Coleman spent the rest of day cleaning out Grandma's cottage, while the men, including Harrison and Spencer, cleared her parents' house of soot and ash and made it liveable again. Other neighbours dropped in with items of clothing and a range of household goods that the Coleman's might need. Their generosity was overwhelming, and the sense of community heart-warming.

147

Cleaning out Grandma's belongings was challenging, with many tears shed between Zoe and Mum, but when Zoe came across a box full of Bible verses lovingly hand-written by Grandma, she had trouble containing herself. She placed the old shoe box on her lap and sat on Grandma's lounge room floor and began reading. Many verses she knew, others she didn't, but all were precious.

"Take it, Zoe." Mum placed her hand gently on Zoe's shoulder as she sat on the lounge chair behind her. "They're precious, aren't they?"

Drawing in a deep breath, Zoe nodded. She lifted a few papers to her nose and breathed in the delicate scent of the paper. Grandma would never be far away now she had this box full of precious treasure.

By late afternoon both houses were in order, and the two families gathered outside under the poinciana tree for a well-deserved drink. The air had cleared of smoke, but the fire had left its mark on the surrounding hills. No longer green or brown, the ground was black, and charred trees stood bare, stripped of all their foliage, naked and totally exposed and standing like stick figures in a kid's cartoon.

Zoe turned to Harrison and took his hand. "Will you stay for Grandma's funeral, Harrison?"

Soft brown eyes lifted to hers, melting her heart. He squeezed her hand. "I'd love to, Zoe. The clinic will survive without me...besides, Spencer's invited me to go up in his plane tomorrow."

Zoe threw her head back and laughed. "You're joking, right?"

Spencer appeared beside her, a smirk on his face. "He's not joking, Zoe. I said I'll take him up to check out the damage."

She raised her eyebrows. "So, do I get an invite?"

"You've had your plane ride, Zoe. Let us have a boys' outing." Spencer's eyes held a twinkle as he held her gaze.

Zoe shook her head, but she couldn't stop chuckling at the turn of events. It'd do Harrison good to spend time with Spencer, and besides, she had a funeral to get ready for.

"Fine. Just look after him."

He waggled his brows. "Of course."

The rest of the evening passed pleasantly. With Dad in hospital, Mr. Coleman, cooked hamburgers and onion on the barbecue with help from Harrison and Spencer. Mum found enough food in the fridge and freezer to feed everybody, and to finish it off, she brought out ice-creams. Thankfully, the back-up generator for the fridges had kicked in when the power went off.

Once the Colemans' left, Zoe and Harrison stayed seated outside in the cool while Mum put Peter to bed.

"I'm glad you're staying, Harrison." Zoe snuggled into his shoulder.

"So am I, Zo." He stroked her hair gently.

"Do you ever think about all this?" Zoe angled her head and gazed up at the sky.

"What do you mean?"

"Like, what it's all about..." She shrugged. "Dad could easily have died out there yesterday. And with Grandma dying..." Zoe's voice caught. Harrison pulled her tighter and kissed her head. "It just makes me realise we never know what's going to happen from one day to the next."

"I hadn't given it much thought, to be honest, but you're right." He brushed her hair with his hand. "I guess we never know."

"No, but God does." Zoe straightened and looked into Harrison's brown eyes. She lifted her hand to his cheek, rubbing her thumb through his stubble. "I don't know what life has in store for us, Harrison, but I want us to do it together, and with God."

Harrison's shoulders fell. "Zoe…"

She lifted a finger to his lips. "Don't say anything. Just think about it?" She angled her head and smiled at him.

He drew a slow breath and turned his gaze to the sky.

Chapter Eighteen

Grandma's funeral was held two days later. The small chapel on top of the hill had been untouched by the fire, but all around were reminders of just how devastating it had been. It seemed all of Bellhaven had turned out for the occasion. Esme Davis had been a well-respected member of the church and was well-known throughout the whole area for her kindness and generosity. But the fire seemed to have tightened the whole community, and even people Mum didn't know turned up to pay their respects.

When Zoe arrived with Harrison shortly before eleven a.m, she greeted the family and friends gathered outside the chapel with a smile, although inside her heart was a mess. Leaning on Harrison's arm, she made her way to the front seat and sat beside Mum, Dad and Peter. Zoe fought hard to hold back her tears as the organist played Grandma's favourite hymn, "Abide with Me". How was she ever going to stand in front of all these people and deliver the eulogy?

She leaned against Harrison as her focus was drawn to the casket at the front. The family had requested no flowers, and instead, donations could be made to help the bush-fire victims. However, one beautiful wreath of white oriental lilies, chrysanthemums, orchids, and roses sat on top of the casket. Tears pricked Zoe's eyes. Grandma would have loved it. As much as Zoe had been dreading saying her final farewell to

Grandma, peace settled on her heart. Death was just a doorway to another world, and Grandma was in a better place. That didn't mean she wouldn't miss Grandma, but having that assurance gave Zoe peace and hope that one day they would be reunited. She squeezed Harrison's hand as the priest stood and moved to the pulpit.

"We're gathered here today to say farewell to Esme June Davis and to commit her into the hands of God. Please join me in singing one of Esme's favourite hymns, 'To God be the Glory'."

Zoe inhaled slowly. As Harrison placed his arm around her shoulder and joined in the singing, she was surprised to hear him singing as if it meant something to him… he hadn't told her too much about what he and Spencer had talked about on their flight the day before, but she sensed a change in him. Not something tangible, but real, nonetheless. God was working in his heart, of that she was sure. She smiled as his voice rang out, "Praise the Lord, praise the Lord, let the earth hear His voice, Praise the Lord, praise the Lord, let the people rejoice. Oh, come to the Father, through Jesus the Son, And give Him the glory, great things He has done."

As the music faded, the priest smiled at the congregation. "Let us pray." Unlike a normal service, everyone remained standing but bowed their heads as the prayer began. As Harrison pulled her tighter, Zoe leaned into him.

"Our Father in heaven, we thank You that through Jesus Christ, You have given us the gift of eternal life, and that nothing, not even death, can separate us from Your love. We thank you for the abundant life You give us here on earth, but we thank You even more for the eternal life which is ours through the death and resurrection of Christ Jesus.

"Esme knew Your love, and lived her life with You as Lord and Saviour. We thank You for her life, and the example she gave us of what it is to live a truly Christian life. As

Ephesians 4, verse 1 says, may we all "live a life worthy of the calling we have received", just like Esme did. Help us in our mourning, and help us to live each day with a heart of gratitude for the life You have given us, to treasure each day, and to be a blessing to those around us, just like Esme was. Give us a living faith in your Son Jesus Christ, who suffered death for our sins, and who rose from the grave to give us hope and a future. Amen."

Zoe dabbed her eyes as she sat. The eulogy was next, and she needed to steady herself. She'd spent most of the last two days preparing what she would say, but now the time had come, God was laying different words on her heart, and so when she moved to the front of the chapel, she put her paper aside and took a deep breath. She swallowed hard, and then smiled at the congregation. So many familiar faces, but also many she didn't know. But Grandma knew them, and they knew her.

"Esme, *Grandma,* was such a precious lady. She was gentle and kind, but had a strength of character that made her a heroine in my eyes. Grandma knew who she was. She was a wife, a mother, a grandmother, but first and foremost, she was a child of God. Grandma's faith in God never wavered, despite times of trial and challenge, of which there were plenty throughout her eighty-three years. She always trusted that God would provide for her and her family, a truth I need to be reminded of again and again. 'God is faithful, Zoe', she would always remind me. 'He knows how many hairs are on your head, He knows your thoughts before you even think them. He loves you, Zoe. He'll take care of you.'

"I had the privilege of having Grandma pray for me whenever she put me to bed when I stayed with her and Grandfather when I was little. I feel bad that I strayed from my faith for a while when I moved to the city to study, but I fully believe it was Grandma's prayers that brought me back. She was my spiritual mentor and guide throughout my growing years, and now, as I embark on my career as a doctor, and I plan my wedding to my fiancé, Harrison, my greatest desire is that I do her proud in all I do, say and think. If I can be half the woman Grandma was, I'll be pleased." Zoe paused and took a deep breath. "There are so many stories I could share, but I'd love my brother, Peter, to come and share his thoughts with you." Zoe shifted her gaze to Peter, and smiled at him. "Peter, come up with me." She held her hand out as he rose from his seat and stepped to the front and stood beside her. "Peter, tell everyone about Grandma."

Zoe put her hand lightly on Peter's shoulder. It was a risk having him here, but it was the right thing to do. Peter wanted to say good-bye to Grandma too.

He stuttered, and turned his head to Zoe.

"It's okay, Peter, whenever you're ready." She smiled at him.

He turned his head to the front. "Grandma's in heaven. She's in heaven with Jesus. She used to tell me stories about heaven and what it would be like. She said it's the best place ever, and that once we're there, we'll be able to see God face to face. Grandma was my friend and I'm going to miss her. She used to make me apple pies and she gave me lolly pops every time I visited. She hugged me when I was upset, and told me Jesus loved me." Tears rolled down his cheeks, and he turned to Zoe. "Zoe, I can't say any more."

She pulled him closer. "It's okay, Peter. "We're all going to miss her. Grandma loved you so much, and she'd be proud that you got up here and told everyone how much she meant to you." Zoe turned her focus back to the congregation. "For those of us who are Christians, we can cling to God's promise of love and hope just like Grandma did. We can look forward to the day when Jesus will return and will take away all pain and suffering. But when we face challenges, just like we did with the bush fire, we need to cling to this hope just as Grandma did. This world can't promise joy and peace and happiness, but God promises these things to all who believe, both here and in heaven. Let's hold onto this hope, just as Esme, *Grandma,* did." She turned to look at the casket and pushed back her tears. "God bless you, Grandma. Go in peace."

She led Peter back to their seats, and as she sat, Harrison took her hand and squeezed it.

Turning her head, she smiled at him. Even though her heart was heavy, she had peace. Grandma's prayers had reached God's ears. Zoe believed her prayers for Harrison had too.

Following the service and the actual burial in the cemetery beside the church, most of the mourners returned to the farm for a light lunch. Mum and Dad had been worried about buying enough food, but Zoe and Harrison had already agreed they'd cover the cost. Zoe had no idea where the money was going to come from to meet all the costs going forward, but she'd decided to trust God. She'd do what she could, and she'd still pursue the bank and the man who'd taken her parents' money, and she'd run some fundraisers, but God would have the final say. If her parents lost the farm, it wouldn't be the end of the world. He'd provide for them. She had no idea how, or what their life would look like, but they'd be okay.

"Zoe, I need to tell you something." Harrison slipped his arm across her shoulder as she poured a cup of tea out of the church's large tea pot they'd borrowed for the occasion.

She looked up, her eyebrows raised. "Now?"

"Yes. It can't wait."

She raised her brows further. "Okay." What was so urgent that he'd take her away from their guests?

He led her around the side of the house and to the back of the shed, and turned her to face him. His eyes held a gentleness she'd only glimpsed occasionally, and as they connected with hers, she somehow knew he was going to tell her something important.

"Zoe, when I was in the plane with Spencer yesterday, I gave my heart to the Lord."

Zoe's eyes widened. Had she heard correctly? "How…" Her mind buzzed, trying to take it in.

"If you shush, I'll tell you." His whole face lit up.

"Okay." She tried to control herself. This was the best news she'd had, ever.

"Can we sit somewhere?"

"How about under that tree over there?" She pointed to a shady spot on the edge of the property.

"Perfect." He placed his arm lightly across her shoulder as they strolled to the tree. "I didn't like him to start with, you probably know that already."

Zoe nodded. That was an understatement.

"Well, he told me he's planning on selling an apartment he has in Singapore and giving all the money to his parents so they can rebuild."

Zoe's eyes widened further. "Really?"

Harrison nodded. "He said not to say anything to them. He's just going to do it and send the money to them anonymously. But it made me think that he wasn't such a bad person after all, and so I asked him why he'd do that. Surely he'd want the money for himself, but he said, no, God had blessed him, and he wanted to help his parents. He didn't need the apartment. He's got staff accommodation out at the base, and he reckons he's got all he needs, and if ever he needed money to buy another place, God would provide. It blew my mind."

Harrison looked at the ground, picking up a piece of dry grass and twiddling it between his fingers. "I always thought God wasn't relevant, He might be okay for the older generation because that's what they'd grown up with, but I'd never really seen someone like Spencer live out his faith in such a real way. I guess there's Ben and Tessa, but I just thought they were being strong in themselves. I didn't realise until now that their strength came from God. So, I asked him to tell me about his faith.

"He said he didn't see the need for God for a long time, even though he'd always believed He existed. When he became a pilot, he began living the high life, partying, drinking, women, you know how it goes." He glanced up. "But gradually he realised it all meant nothing. His life was empty and had no meaning. So he stopped going to parties, and started reading his Bible. All the passages he'd read when he was younger started coming to life, and in a hotel room in New York he gave his life to the Lord. He promised God that he'd serve Him in whatever way He directed, and that's when he joined the Flying Doctor Service. He wanted to give, not take, just like Jesus did. He explained that Jesus had given His life so that all those who believe in Him can also live. He didn't have to, but he chose to, and that by doing so, we can now live with God's love in our lives, and it's His love we can show to others."

Harrison lifted his head and met Zoe's gaze. "You probably know all of this, Zoe, but the way Spencer spoke, I knew he meant it. He wasn't putting it on, I just knew it was true. Something happened inside me up there in that plane, like blinders being removed from my eyes, and I started to cry."

Zoe reached out and squeezed his hand, wiping tears from her own eyes. She'd been praying for this day, but now it was here, she could barely believe it had happened. To hear Harrison talking like this was just beyond her wildest dreams.

"He asked me if I'd like to ask Jesus into my life, and I said yes. He led me in a prayer, and I asked Jesus to forgive my sins, and to be my Lord and Saviour." He smiled a smile that reached deep within Zoe, filling her with such joy she thought she would burst.

"I'm so happy to hear that, Harrison." She returned his smile and wrapped her arms around him, hugging him, pulling him close. After a while, she lifted her head. "Why didn't you tell me when you came back?"

Harrison brushed her face as he gazed into her eyes. "I'm not really sure. You were busy writing your speech, and I think I just needed some time to digest it all."

She smiled at him again. "It doesn't matter. This is the best news you could have given me."

He chuckled. "I thought it might be. I don't know why I was being so stubborn. Maybe I just didn't like being pushed."

Zoe drew back. "I didn't push you."

He lifted his hand and touched her cheek. "No, but I had you, your mum and my mum all praying for me, and probably my dad, so if that's not pressure, I don't know what is."

Zoe laughed. "It must have been God's sense of humour putting you together with Spencer."

"He's a cool dude. I can see why you fell for him, Zoe."

"But not as cool as you, Harrison."

He smiled at her. "Just as well." He angled his head as a cheeky grin grew on his face. "So does this mean we can set a date?"

Zoe laughed. "You didn't do this just so I would, did you?"

Pretend shock played on his face. "As if I'd do something like that!" His expression grew serious. "Absolutely not, Zoe. I meant what I prayed, I know God's living in me. I feel different." He paused, drawing a breath. "I've got a lot to learn, but I'm looking forward to experiencing it all with you." He took her hand, gently rubbing his thumb over her skin as his brown eyes looked deeply into hers. "Zoe, I love you with all my heart, and now I have God's love in my heart too, I can't think of anything I want to do more than share my life with you. I'd love to marry you right now, but if you need to wait until the end of the year, I'll wait as long as you need."

"Oh Harrison, that's so sweet." She wiped her eyes and swallowed hard. Harrison's gentleness and willingness to delay their marriage softened Zoe's heart even further. "If I could make it sooner I would, but how about we make it out here, two weeks after I finish? As long as the bank hasn't taken the farm by then."

Harrison chuckled. "Don't you worry about that, Zoe— they won't have."

She drew her eyebrows together. "What do you know that I don't?"

"Spencer was going to tell you… but I guess I can. He found that guy, and he reckons your parents will have a good case against him."

"Really?" This was too much.

Harrison nodded. "Yes, but that's not all. I was thinking I'll sell my apartment and buy a cheaper house, maybe near my parents, and I'll give the difference to your parents to help cover their mortgage."

"Did Spencer put you up to that?"

Harrison chuckled. "No, but he gave me the idea."

"But you love your apartment."

"But I love you and your parents more."

Zoe's eyes welled with tears. "Harrison, that is so kind and generous."

"Well, we can't take it with us, and you encouraged everyone to be more like your Grandma, so…" He drew a breath, but she didn't let him exhale. Closing the distance between them, she kissed him slowly as her heart overflowed with love for him.

Leaving Mum, Dad and Peter two days later, Zoe promised them that she and Harrison would do everything they could to ensure the mortgage repayments on the farm were made until things improved. Harrison didn't want her parents to know about his decision to sell the apartment. "Let's just keep that between ourselves, Zoe", he'd said to her later on the day of Grandma's funeral. Zoe had been so touched by that act of humility. God had really changed Harrison's heart already and given him a more genuine care and concern for others. He'd even offered to take Peter for another drive in his car and had played chess with him until the wee hours of the morning.

As she drove down the driveway behind Harrison's sports car, Zoe waved until Mum, Dad and Peter were out of sight. She'd been tempted to leave her car behind and drive with Harrison, but she'd need it once back in the city, and so they had to drive the whole way in separate cars.

The next few months were going to be demanding. Apart from starting her Internship, Spencer had given them the details of the man who'd taken her parents' money. Harrison had offered to help her mount a legal case against the man on their behalf. One of his friends was a lawyer who specialized in cases like this, and Harrison was confident Brent would take it on. And of course, there was a wedding to plan!

Driving through Bellhaven, Zoe sent up a prayer for all the local folk. They'd been through so much, and still there was no rain in sight. One of the verses in Grandma's box came to mind… *"So do not worry, saying, 'What shall we eat?' or 'What shall we drink?' or 'What shall we wear?' For the pagans run after all these things, and your heavenly Father knows that you need them. But seek first his kingdom and his righteousness, and all these things will be given to you as well".*

Yes, Lord, please help me to seek You first, and please help the folk out here not to worry. It must be so hard when they see their land burned and parched, and their cattle hungry and thin, but help them to trust that Your provision will be sufficient. Make them stronger because of the hardships they've endured, and provide rain for them in Your time, dear Lord. And bless Harrison. My heart's still overflowing with gratitude to You for touching his life and drawing him into Your Kingdom. Let him grow closer to You each day, and become the man of God You want him to be. Please help me to trust You, dear Lord, and not to rely on my own strength as I'm prone to do. You're my rock, my stronghold. You're my God and I praise You. May Your goodness and love follow me all the days of my life, just like it did Grandma. Blessed be the name of the Lord. Amen.

Switching on the CD player, Zoe slipped in the new CD Spencer had given her just before she left—a Praise and Worship collaboration he said would uplift her on the long drive home. He also gave one to Harrison. She turned the volume up and listened to the songs, joining in as the words became familiar. Spencer was right—the whole CD was uplifting, and by the time she arrived home, her heart was fully open to God leading and guiding her in the months ahead.

Chapter Nineteen

Later that year

"Harrison, did you see the forecast?" Zoe leaned across and kissed Harrison on the cheek as she jumped into his new car. Well, not new, just new for him. After they returned from the farm, he not only sold his apartment, but he also sold his fancy convertible and bought a cheaper and more practical car and put the difference towards Zoe's parents' mortgage payments.

"No, I didn't, but let me guess…it's going to rain?"

Zoe chuckled. "Yes. How did you know?"

"Because you've never been so excited about a weather forecast before."

"Right." She clicked on her seatbelt and smiled at him. "But do you know *where* it's going to rain?"

He lifted his finger to his mouth and raised his brow. "Bellhaven?"

She chuckled as she nodded. "Yes!! At last! Rain's been forecast for the whole area. Praise God."

"That's great… as long as it stops before the wedding."

She laughed. "Oh well, I guess a bit of mud never hurt anyone."

"Unless they're wearing a white wedding dress."

She grimaced. "That's true. But anyway, it doesn't matter. It just means there might be grass instead of dirt."

Harrison smiled at her. "Always look on the bright side, hey Zoe?"

"Better than the opposite."

"You're right, and there's nothing we can do about it now, anyway. All my family are getting ready to head out there. I hope Bellhaven's ready for them."

Zoe laughed. "Everybody's looking forward to it. It's kind of like a celebration party now all the properties have been rebuilt and everything's almost back to normal after the fire."

"A real country shin-dig! I'm looking forward to it."

"And so am I, Harrison. One week to go…I can't wait!" She slipped her hand onto his leg and rested her head back against the car seat. "Do you mind if I catch a bit of sleep? Last night's shift was a killer."

"Go ahead. I'll wake you when we get there."

She smiled at him before lowering the back of her seat and closing her eyes.

Harrison glanced at Zoe sleeping beside him as they headed out to the farm to prepare for their wedding, and let out a contented sigh. It had been such a long wait, and the year had been hard on her, but she'd done it. Zoe was now a fully qualified doctor, having completed all her rotations successfully, and now she had a month off for their wedding and honeymoon. It was hard to believe it was finally happening. He just hoped his sisters would arrive from England in time, not like last year when they almost didn't make it for Christmas because of a blizzard. A pity Angus and Alastair couldn't make it, but at least Chloe and Sophie would be there with Lara-Katie and Lachlan. And of course, Mum and Dad were coming out, as were Ben and Tessa, and Jayden and their new little baby girl, Naomi, and Tessa's parents, Telford and Eleanor. As well as half their church… He hoped Bellhaven was going to cope.

In many ways it would have been easier to have had the wedding in the city, but Zoe had been adamant she wanted to get married on the farm, especially now her parents had been successful in getting most of their money back and the farm was safe, so everyone was making a weekend of it. To be honest, he really didn't care. He just wanted to marry her. God had blessed him so much by bringing her into his life, and now he couldn't imagine living without her.

And this year they'd grown so much closer, even though Zoe was working long hours. They'd spent lots of quality time together, talking, reading, studying the Bible, praying, as well as snatching time for the occasional trip to the beach to unwind. It had been on one of those trips that Zoe had surprised him with the best birthday present he could have wished for…a swim with the dolphins at Sea World, something he'd wanted to do for a long time.

Up ahead, clouds appeared and were darkening by the minute. Maybe Zoe had been right and it was going to rain. He shook his head. God really had a sense of humour. All year they'd been praying for rain, and it just had to come this week of all weeks. But the farmers needed it more than ever, so he wasn't going to complain. At least there wouldn't be another fire.

Zoe stirred beside him and looked up with sleepy eyes. "Are we almost there?"

"Two more hours. Do you want to stop?"

"No, just keep driving." She turned over and went back to sleep.

He placed his hand gently on her back as she slept. It would have been nice to talk with her, but just being with her

164

was enough. He increased the volume on his iPhone and listened to Pastor Stanthorpe's latest sermon again.

Two hours later he pulled into Bellrae's driveway. He rubbed her back. "Zoe, we're here. Wake up."

Her eyes flickered then opened before she sat with a start. "It's raining!" She rubbed her eyes and peered outside. "Ha! Look at the puddles!"

"I know. It's a deluge. We don't even have an umbrella in the car."

"It doesn't matter. I'm happy to get wet."

"Okay." His eyes met hers and his breath caught. She looked so beautiful with her hair all messed up, tumbling carelessly down her back and neck. He reached out and pulled her close, cupping his hands around her face, his eyes taking in not only her physical beauty, but the beauty of her inner being. "I love you, Zoe." He smiled at her before lowering his lips and kissing her gently.

Hard knocking on the car window made him pull away. He glanced outside. Peter stood in the rain holding a large umbrella, a huge smile on his face. Harrison chuckled. This was the start. A week of activity lay ahead of them, but in one week, he and Zoe would be married. And that's all that mattered.

The week passed not like they'd planned. For one, it rained. Not just normal rain, but heavy, torrential, flooding rain. In fact, there was talk of mass evacuations if it didn't let up. Zoe decided she'd take it all in her stride, but they started making contingency plans for the wedding in case it didn't ease.

On Friday morning, Zoe woke to sunshine streaming in through her bedroom window, warming her face. She sat up and smiled. She wouldn't have complained if it had still been raining, but God had chosen, for whatever reason, to make it stop. The ground would have time to dry out, and everything would be fine. It also meant all their guests could arrive safely.

She slipped out of bed and quickly changed into a pair of shorts and t-shirt. Before all the family arrived, she had one thing she wanted to do. Sneaking out the side door, she headed to the shed and pulled out a push-bike. Climbing onto it, she rode down the driveway towards Grandma's cottage.

The cottage sat on a small incline, and by the time she got there, Zoe was puffing. Despite her resolution earlier in the year to run and ride every day, because of her demanding schedule she hadn't kept to it, and now she was paying the price. Plus, it was Harrison's old bike he'd given Peter when he got his new one.

The sun was higher here, and it bounced off the mist covering the valley below. The rain had cleaned the ground and the air, and everything looked crisp and fresh. To Zoe's surprise, one of Grandma's rose bushes had survived the heavy rain of the last few days, and a beautiful deep-red rosebud had begun to open. She walked towards it and carefully picked it, and as she held it to her nose, the perfume invoked fond memories of Grandma.

She walked to the front steps and sat on the middle one. The tranquillity of the surroundings wrapped itself around her and brought calmness to her soul as she took in not only the beauty of the early morning, but the wonder of God's creation all around her, including the beautiful, perfectly formed rosebud in her hand.

Taking a piece of paper from her pocket, she opened it and smiled. Grandma's Bible verses had given her strength and encouragement throughout the year, and had helped keep her heart and mind focused on God. Today's verse was no different...Psalm 37, verse 4, *"Take delight in the Lord, and He will give you the desires of your heart.*" Her heart swelled. Yes, God had indeed given her the desires of her heart. Harrison's faith had blossomed this year, and he'd not only become involved in the church, he'd been a regular at the Bible Study Ben had started when he and Tessa returned from Ecuador, and had grown in leaps and bounds. His hunger and thirst for the word had amazed her, and had warmed her heart so much. She was sure Grandma would now approve of her choice of a marriage partner, but her heart was sad Grandma wouldn't see her married. But being here, sitting on Grandma's front steps, with one of Grandma's favourite roses in her hand, brought Grandma close again.

Zoe sniffed the bud and smiled. "Thanks, Grandma, for your wise words, and for praying for me all those years. As Harrison and I marry tomorrow, I know you'll be watching from heaven, and I hope you'll be smiling." As she stood, she placed the rosebud on the step. "Grandma, this is for you. I love you."

As she rode slowly back down to the farmhouse, Zoe took a moment to breathe in the crisp, clean air, and thanked God for His love and faithfulness. Mum and Dad were able to keep the farm, but somehow she knew that if they'd lost it, she would have been okay with it. *Your will, Your way, Your time, dear Lord. Please help me to remember this, every moment of every day.*

By lunch time, their wedding guests began arriving. Margaret and Harold, Chloe and Sophie, the children, Ben and Tessa, Jayden and baby Naomi, and Tessa's parents all arrived together. Thankfully they weren't staying at the farmhouse, but the plan was for them to spend the afternoon there before going to either Grandma's cottage or the Coleman's new house, which, thanks to Spencer's generosity, had been fitted out as a B & B.

Harrison slipped his arm around Zoe's shoulder as they greeted their guests. Throughout the afternoon they managed to share just a few moments alone, but they both knew they had a lifetime together to look forward to, God willing, and having all their family here was such a special time.

They'd set up tables and chairs under the Poinciana tree and everyone based themselves there for the afternoon, although Dad and Harrison took the men on a tour of the property while the ladies just enjoyed each other's company. Zoe had become friendly with Tessa since she'd returned from overseas, and would miss her friendship when she and Ben moved to their own property in a matter of days, although Tessa had said that she and Harrison were welcome to visit whenever they wanted.

Ben and Tessa's baby girl was just gorgeous, with her beautifully formed face and tiny rosebud mouth that reminded Zoe of the rosebud she'd left on Grandma's step just that morning. When Zoe did her rotation in the maternity ward, she'd started thinking about whether she wanted children of her own. Harrison did, but she'd have to give it more thought. In the meantime, she was happy just holding this precious little bundle.

As Zoe watched Mum talking with Margaret and Eleanor, she smiled at how she and Harrison had somehow managed to still plan their own wedding despite all three women wanting to be involved. She looked down as Lachlan came up to her and gazed at the baby. "She's pretty." He touched her little hand and looked up with a bright face. "Mummy's getting one of these soon."

Chloe burst out laughing. "I've still got a while to go, Lachy."

"You're very lucky," Zoe said to the little boy.

"I know. Mummy said I can be her helper."

"And I'm sure you'll do a great job." Zoe's heart warmed. Yes, maybe she would like to have children. But first, she had a wedding and then a honeymoon, and then she was starting her new job at the P.A. Hospital. It would happen in God's time, not hers.

Later, Zoe slipped her arm around Harrison's waist as the sun set below the horizon, casting the sky in brilliant oranges and pinks, and led him away from the crowd.

"One more day, Miss Taylor." He nuzzled her neck, sending goose-bumps down her spine.

She turned to face him, lifting her lips to his. "I can't wait, Harrison."

Chapter Twenty

The day of the wedding promised to be a perfect summer's day... hot, but not too hot. Zoe was thankful, but to be honest, she would have been happy marrying Harrison in a blizzard or a heat wave. Since he'd given his heart to the Lord, she'd just fallen deeper in love with him every day, and she couldn't wait to be his wife.

She sat up in bed and opened her Bible, taking out another of Grandma's verses. Today of all days she wanted God to speak to her heart, to give her a message for this most important of days; the day she was to marry her true love.

She unfolded the piece of paper. Grandma's verse for today was Colossians 3, verses 12 to 15: *"Therefore, as God's chosen people, holy and dearly loved, clothe yourselves with compassion, kindness, humility, gentleness and patience. Bear with each other and forgive one another if any of you has a grievance against someone. Forgive as the Lord forgave you. And over all these virtues put on love, which binds them all together in perfect unity. Let the peace of Christ rule in your hearts, since as members of one body you were called to peace. And be thankful."*

What better verses to prepare her for her marriage? *Clothe yourselves with compassion, kindness, humility, gentleness and patience. The fruit of the spirit. And over all these put on love, which binds them all together in perfect unity.*

Lord God, please let these virtues be evident in my life. Let me be kind and gentle with Harrison, compassionate and caring, patient and loving. Lord, bless our marriage, and let me be the wife Harrison needs and wants. Amen.

Zoe spent another few minutes reading the Word and praying before rising and showering. Savouring the warmth of the water as it flowed over her body, she stayed in the shower slightly longer than normal now the water tanks were full after the rain. God was indeed good.

Tessa and Emma, her two attendants, were due to arrive at seven o'clock for a leisurely breakfast before the hairdresser and beautician were due to arrive at eight-thirty. The ceremony was late morning, and the decision had been made to hold it where Zoe had always wanted it, under the lemon scented gum trees. The ground would continue drying today, and the trees would provide ample shade from the heat of the day. An added bonus, the creek was flowing, and men from the community had set up everything for the ceremony and reception yesterday, and it all looked great! She was so excited.

Tessa and Emma arrived right on time. Tessa had brought Naomi with her, and Mum immediately offered to look after her. The way she held the tiny baby girl made Zoe think she'd be a wonderful grandmother, just like her own.

Zoe led Tessa and Emma out onto the new deck, courtesy of an anonymous donor. Zoe had her suspicions, but neither Spencer nor Harrison had owned up to it, but Mum and Dad were ecstatic. Now they had somewhere to eat other than their cramped kitchen, which now had air-conditioning, much to Zoe's surprise.

"Well girls, we have our own personal waiter this morning..." She held her arm out and looked towards the door.

Peter, wearing dark pants and a white shirt, and a huge grin on his face, stepped forward and stood beside Zoe.

"Peter's going to be looking after us. He's made us some delicious treats, so sit back and enjoy!" Zoe gave him a big hug before pulling out a chair and taking a seat around the large timber table he and Dad had made together recently.

"This is lovely, Zoe," Emma said as she placed some pieces of tropical fruit onto her plate, her blue eyes lighting up her petite face.

Zoe smiled fondly at her flat-mate. How she'd miss living with Emma after sharing the past four years with her. "Thanks, Em. I'm so glad you both could come out."

"We wouldn't have missed it for the world, would we, Tessa?"

Tessa shook her head. "Absolutely not."

"Would you like some coffee?" Peter stood beside the table with a coffee pot in his hand.

"That would be lovely, thanks Peter." Tessa smiled up at him as she held her cup out.

"Zoe's getting married today." The grin on Peter's face stretched from ear to ear.

"It's exciting, isn't it, Peter?" Tessa smiled at him as he poured her coffee.

"Yes, and she saved the farm."

"I know, she's a very clever girl."

Zoe caught Tessa's eyes and let out a small laugh. For Peter's sake she was glad the farm had been saved, but it wasn't her doing, it was God's. She knew that. Yes, maybe she and Harrison and Spencer had been the instruments God had used, but she had no doubt that God was to be given all the praise and glory, not her.

"Grandma can't come. She's in heaven with Jesus."

"But she's here in spirit, Peter. Look, I'm going to wear Grandma's brooch today in my hair." Zoe, opened the box sitting on the table and pulled out a beautiful dainty rhinestone vintage brooch, studded with five ivory pearls, remodelled into a hair comb.

"That's Grandma's, Zoe. It's pretty."

"It is, isn't it?"

"Yes. Do you want anything else to eat?"

"No, thanks, Peter, this is wonderful, thank you."

"It's my pleasure, Zoe." He giggled as he left and went back into the kitchen.

"He's a lovely boy, Zoe." Tessa said as she sipped her coffee.

"Yes, he really is."

The next hour passed pleasantly, and right on time, a car came up the driveway and stopped in front of the house. The hairdresser and beautician climbed out and waved to Zoe.

Zoe stood and waved down at the girls, both dressed in hippy-type summer dresses and returned the wave. "Come on up, Piper, Heidi. Peter can get your gear."

Moments later, Piper and Heidi appeared on the deck, with Peter not far behind carrying their bags.

"What a lovely deck, Zoe." Piper bent down and hugged her.

"Yes, it's lovely sitting out here. Thanks for coming out, both of you." Zoe returned Piper's hug and squeezed Heidi's hand.

"Our pleasure, Zoe. We're looking forward to it."

Zoe introduced Piper and Heidi to Emma and Tessa, and offered them a seat. "Help yourselves to some food, and then we'd better get started."

For the next few hours, Piper and Heidi pampered the three girls. Mum occasionally came out with Naomi still safely ensconced in her arms. Tessa fed her once, but then Mum was eager to have her back. Piper was going to do her hair after she'd finished with the girls.

"Well, what do you think?" Piper held a large mirror in front of Zoe.

Zoe's eyes widened as she looked at her reflection. She hadn't wanted anything too different, but she loved what she saw. Lifting her hand to the soft chignon sitting above her left shoulder, she smiled. Harrison would love it. So soft and shiny, and Grandma's brooch topped it off superbly.

She gave Piper and Heidi grateful smiles. "I love it. Thank you so much."

"You look beautiful, Zoe." Tessa gave her a warm smile.

"You look pretty good yourself, Tessa." Tessa's light brown hair had been curled and bounced lightly on her shoulders.

She laughed. "It's been a while since I've been pampered like this. We should do it more often."

"We can always dream." Zoe chuckled. Where would she find two hours to pamper herself once she returned to work?"

They all turned as Mum stepped onto the deck with a crying Naomi in her arms. "I think she wants her mum."

Tessa cooed at the baby as she took her from Mum's arms, and Naomi instantly stopped. Amazing.

Shortly after, while Naomi slept, Tessa, Emma and Mum helped Zoe into her dress, a sweetheart design in lace and French tulle over lustre satin. As she slipped it on and stood in the middle of Mum's bedroom floor while Emma did up the twenty tiny buttons on the back, it really started to feel like she was getting married.

"There, don't you look a treat." Mum's eyes moistened as she stepped back to get a better look. "Grandma would be proud." Mum held both her arms out and pulled Zoe into a gentle hug. "She loved you so much, Zoe."

It was all Zoe could do to stop her tears from flowing. Although Grandma wasn't here, her sweet nature lived on in

Mum, and Zoe had a sense Grandma might be smiling down on her from above.

Harrison knew it was time when Jayden and his new friend, Luke, began playing the song that he and Zoe had chosen for her walk through the gum trees. He drew in a deep breath and caught the eyes of both Ben and Spencer. What would he have done without them today? Until this morning he had no nervousness at all, but a switch had been flicked in his stomach, and the butterflies had been with him all day. He had no doubt Zoe would turn up, he was as sure of her love as he was of his for her. Maybe it was normal...Ben said it was, but he didn't like it. But now as he turned and waited for the first glimpse of his beautiful bride, a sense of anticipation flowed through him. This was it. He was going to marry his Zoe. After all the waiting, his dreams were becoming reality.

A car door closed, and soon after, Peter appeared through the trees holding Lachlan's and Lara-Katie's hands. They could have just been taking a stroll in a forest park, except for what they wore—long black pants, waistcoats and bow-ties for the boys, and the cutest white dress he'd ever seen for Lara-Katie. She held a small basket overflowing with baby's breath and delicate salmon rosebuds.

Following close behind, Emma looked like a princess in a dark blue, soft flowing mid-length dress. And then came Tessa. Harrison glanced at Ben—the smile on Ben's face said it all. Tessa looked the epitome of elegance in her dark blue dress as she stepped slowly through the trees to the beautiful music Ben and Tessa's teenage son, Jayden, and his new friend, Luke, were playing.

Harrison's heart beat faster and his breath caught as Zoe appeared through the trees with her arm linked through

Kevin's. Never had he seen such beauty. Her face radiated the joy he felt at seeing her, a joy he knew that was so much greater because they both had God in their hearts. And her dress...absolutely perfect for her. Soft, flowing, feminine. He swallowed the lump in his throat as she drew closer. He couldn't take his eyes off her. And then she was in front of him, and Kevin placed her hand into his. He squeezed it and smiled into her beautiful face. He tucked her hand into the crook of his arm as they turned to face Pastor Stanthorpe.

It was like a dream. Pastor Stanthorpe, Harrison and Zoe's pastor from their church in Brisbane, welcomed everyone to the wedding of Harrison James Smith and Zoe Anne Taylor. He thanked God for the beautiful setting, and for bringing the two of them together. They sang their favourite hymn, "Great is Thy Faithfulness," and then he spoke to them. What he was saying was important, so Harrison forced himself to focus, although he just wanted to say "I do".

"Harrison, Zoe, marriage isn't man's invention, it's God's, and its purpose is to honour Him and to bring Him glory. As in all of life, what matters most in marriage is God. You both stand here today declaring your commitment to God and to each other, and I'm honoured to be leading this service today. You both have incredible strengths that you bring to this marriage, and you both have a desire to submit yourself to God's word and to allow God to change you and mould you to become more like Jesus. Thus I'm honoured to be here today as your pastor, to be the one leading this service.

"It's been a blessing seeing you both grow so much this year, and I'm overjoyed that God has brought you to this moment, and that you asked me to be part of your special day. Let's pray."

Harrison squeezed Zoe's hand and caught her eye before bowing his head, the tenderness in her smile sending warmth through his whole body.

176

"Lord, we thank you that You've brought us here to this very moment on this very day. We love Harrison and Zoe and we're excited for them. We pray, Lord, that this commitment being made today would honour and glorify You for their lifetime. May the message of the gospel be evident in this marriage and may they together be true witnesses to Your love to those around them. Oh, Lord, we pray these things in Jesus' name. Amen."

"Tessa is now going to bring us our Bible reading."

Tessa stepped to the middle, in front of the simple arbour of rustic timber doors decorated with a trailing wreath of soft roses. She stood behind a small lectern and cleared her voice. "Today's reading comes from 1 Corinthians 13, verses 1 to 13." She looked down at her Bible and began. *"If I speak in the tongues of men or of angels, but do not have love, I am only a resounding gong or a clanging cymbal. If I have the gift of prophecy and can fathom all mysteries and all knowledge, and if I have a faith that can move mountains, but do not have love, I am nothing. If I give all I possess to the poor and give over my body to hardship that I may boast, but do not have love, I gain nothing.*

"Love is patient, love is kind. It does not envy, it does not boast, it is not proud. It does not dishonour others, it is not self-seeking, it is not easily angered, it keeps no record of wrongs. Love does not delight in evil but rejoices with the truth. It always protects, always trusts, always hopes, always perseveres. Love never fails."

Harrison's heart quickened as the words reached deep into his soul. Life giving words from the Father, and right there he committed to love Zoe with everything he had.

Tessa finished reading… *"And now these three remain: faith, hope and love. But the greatest of these is love."*

Lifting her head, she turned to Harrison and Zoe and gave them a smile that came from deep within. "God bless you both, my dear friends."

They'd written their own vows, and as Harrison took Zoe's hand in his and looked deep into her eyes, he knew this was the moment that he'd been waiting for all his life. He smiled into her beautiful eyes. "James 1, verse 17 says that every good and perfect gift comes from above, and Zoe, you're truly a gift from God and I promise to spend the rest of my life treating you as such. I'll cherish you always and never take you for granted. I'll lead and guide you as Christ leads me. I'll follow His teachings and obey His commands. I'll lead by example, with patience, and with understanding. I'll be slow to anger, and quick to listen. I'll be a strong spiritual leader in our home through good times and bad, in joy and in sorrow." Pausing, he sucked in a steadying breath. "Zoe, I promise to love you and to be faithful to you alone from this day forward until God calls us home. This is my solemn pledge to you and to God." He took the ring from Ben and smiled into her eyes. "Zoe, please accept this ring as a symbol of our covenant and my eternal love for you."

Zoe's eyes misted over as Harrison slipped the white gold wedding band on her finger. And then it was her turn. As Zoe took his hand and smiled into his eyes as she promised to love and honour him as her husband for as long as they both should live, Harrison could hardly contain the joy bubbling inside him. And when Pastor Stanthorpe announced they were man and wife and he could kiss her, he felt giddy with happiness. Zoe was now his wife, and he was the happiest man alive.

Taking her in his arms, he lowered his mouth against hers and kissed her with all the love in his heart. Everyone laughed and cheered, and when he finally pulled back from their kiss, love sparkled from her eyes and reached into his soul.

Soft piano music played in the background while they signed the register under the branches of the scented gum trees. It all seemed like a dream to Zoe as they smiled for the cameras and kissed and laughed again and again. But when Pastor Stanthorpe stood and introduced them as Mr. and Mrs. Harrison Smith, she knew it wasn't a dream.

The reception was held under a large white marquee set up in a nearby paddock. Rows of tables were decorated beautifully but simply with a range of local native flowers and candles. The luncheon, provided by a local catering company, featured a selection of gourmet finger food followed by a choice of grilled salmon, seasoned with garlic, lemon and butter and served with steamed broccolini, and a baby rack of lamb coated with a blend of herbs and spices, and served with sautéed baby carrots and potato croquettes.

All through the afternoon, Zoe could barely keep her eyes off her husband, so handsome in his navy suit, and a smile on his face that warmed her heart, but she did have time to notice that Spencer and Emma were spending a lot of time together…it made her smile—they'd make a perfect couple!

When it came time to leave, Zoe slipped her arm around Harrison's waist while he thanked everyone for coming. As her gaze slowly moved around their family and friends, overwhelming gratitude to God welled up within her for their love and support. But she couldn't wait to be alone with Harrison.

They said their good-byes, and everyone followed them out onto the paddock where a plane sat waiting for them. Spencer stood at the bottom of the steps, his blue eyes twinkling and a grin on his face as wide as the brim of her father's straw hat. As he ushered them up, Zoe smiled at him. He'd always be her friend, and she'd be forever grateful that he'd been the one to lead Harrison to the Lord, but Harrison was the man she'd love forever.

Pausing on the top step, Harrison placed his arm around Zoe's shoulders and tilted her face to his, lowering his lips to hers in a kiss that made everyone clap and cheer. Together they waved to the gathered crowd before ducking their heads and climbing into the back of the small plane, ready for Spencer to fly them to their secret honeymoon destination.

As the plane lifted above the crowd, the vast expanse of the region came into view. Paddocks and hills so badly scarred by the fire were now tinged with green. In God's way and time, the land was recovering.

Zoe laughed with Harrison as they turned and looked back at the "Just Married" sign flapping in the sky behind them before Harrison turned Zoe's face to his, and closing the gap between them, kissed her with unbridled passion.

Know therefore that the Lord your God is God; He is the faithful God, keeping His covenant of love to a thousand generations of those who love Him and keep His commandments. Deuteronomy 7:9

Note From the Author

Hi! It's Juliette here. I hope you enjoyed reading about Harrison's and Zoe's somewhat rocky road to the altar, and their developing relationship with God, the creator and source of love.

Make sure you don't miss updates on any new releases by joining my mailing list if you haven't already done so. You'll also get exclusive sneak previews. It's easy to join, and I promise I won't spam you! Just visit **www.julietteduncan.com/subscribe** to join, and as a thank you for signing up, you'll also receive a **free short story**.

Lastly, could I also ask a favor of you? Reviews help people decide whether to buy a book or not, so could you spare a moment and leave a short review? It doesn't need to be long - just a sentence or two about what you thought of the book would be great, and very much appreciated.

Best regards,

Juliette

Connect with Juliette:

Website: www.julietteduncan.com

Facebook: www.facebook.com/JulietteDuncanAuthor

Twitter: https://twitter.com/Juliette_Duncan

OTHER BOOKS BY JULIETTE DUNCAN

The True Love Series

Book 1: Tender Love
Book 2: Tested Love
Book 3: Tormented Love
Book 4: Triumphant Love
Other related books:
True Love at Christmas
Promises of Love

After her long-term relationship falls apart, Tessa Scott is left questioning God's plan for her life, and is feeling vulnerable and unsure of how to move forward. Ben Williams is struggling to keep the pieces of his life together after his wife of fourteen years walks out on him and their teenage son. Stephanie, Tessa's housemate, knows the pain both Tessa and Ben have suffered. When she inadvertently sets up a meeting between them, there's no denying that they are drawn to each other, but will that mutual attraction do more harm than good? Can Tessa and Ben let go of their leftover baggage and examine their feelings in order to follow a new path? Are they prepared for the road ahead, regardless of the challenges? Will they trust God to equip them with all they need for the journey ahead?

The Shadows Trilogy

Book 1: Lingering Shadows
Book 2: Facing the Shadows
Book 3: Beyond the Shadows

The Shadows Trilogy - A story of passion, love, and of God's inexplicable desire to free people from pasts that haunt them, so they can live a life full of His peace, love and forgiveness, regardless of the circumstances. Set in the UK, The Shadows Trilogy follows the story of Lizzy, a headstrong teacher who has had her heart broken when her minister beau suddenly broke off their relationship without any real reason, and Daniel, a young Irish rogue who steals her heart. Earthy and real, readers will be touched by the raw emotion of their story as God leads them through the challenges they face both as a couple and as individuals.

Secrets and Sacrifice – The Shadows Trilogy Sequel

When Grace O'Connor arrives in the Scottish Highlands, she's hiding a secret and trailing more baggage than she cares to admit. Grace's sister, Brianna, has a history linked to Grace's secret. There, amongst the rugged Scottish Highlands and a community of caring, loving Christians, Grace meets the handsome Ryan MacGregor, an ex-military Paratrooper with a history of his own.

The Madeleine Richards Series

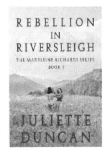  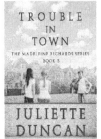 

Although the 3 book series is intended mainly for pre-teen/Tweenage girls, it's been read and enjoyed by people of all ages. Here's what one reader had to say about it: *"Juliette has a fabulous way of bringing her characters to life. Maddy is at typical teenager with authentic views and actions that truly make it feel like you are feeling her pain and angst. You want to enter into her situation and make everything better. Mom and soon to be dad respond to her with love and gentle persuasion while maintaining their faith and trust in Jesus, whom they know, will give them wisdom as they continue on their lives journey. Appropriate for teenage readers but any age can enjoy."* Amazon Reader

All three books are available in both digital and paperback versions. www.julietteduncan.com/series/the-madeleine-richards-series/

 **Hank and Sarah - A Love Story,** the Prequel to *"The Madeleine Richards Series"* is a FREE thank you gift for joining my mailing list. You will also be the first to hear about my next books and get exclusive sneak previews.

Visit www.julietteduncan.com/subscribe

Made in the USA
Middletown, DE
21 February 2019